A Song for St Nicholas

(The Christmas Choir)

Jo Bartlett

Typesetting and Design Fabrian Books – fabrianbooks.com.

About the Author

Jo writes romance and women's fiction in the pockets of time she finds between her day jobs, as a leadership writer and university lecturer, and family life. Jo lives with her husband, four children and four dogs on the Kent coast, so far to the south east of England that they're very nearly French.

Jo is one tenth of the Write Romantics, and is published by Fabrian Books, So Vain Books, DC Thomson, Ulverscoft, Oakhill Press and Recorded Books, and still can't quite believe she's had nine books published. It took a brush with cancer to finally make Jo take the time to sit down and write that first book and it's now her biggest ambition to drink tea and make stuff up on a full time basis.

You can find out more about Jo at:
www.jobartlettauthor.com

Other books by this author

The St Nicholas Bay Series

Somebody Else's Boy
The Gift of Christmas Yet to Come

Fabrian Books' Feel-Good Novels

A Holly Bay Christmas
A Highland Practice
The Christmas Shop at Central Park

The Channel View Farm Series

Give Me Your Answer Do
Second Chances at Channel View Farm

So Vain Books

Among A Thousand Stars

About the Author

Jo writes romance and women's fiction in the pockets of time she finds between her day jobs, as a leadership writer and university lecturer, and family life. Jo lives with her husband, four children and four dogs on the Kent coast, so far to the south east of England that they're very nearly French.

Jo is one tenth of the Write Romantics, and is published by Fabrian Books, So Vain Books, DC Thomson, Ulverscoft, Oakhill Press and Recorded Books, and still can't quite believe she's had nine books published. It took a brush with cancer to finally make Jo take the time to sit down and write that first book and it's now her biggest ambition to drink tea and make stuff up on a full time basis.

You can find out more about Jo at:
www.jobartlettauthor.com

Other books by this author

The St Nicholas Bay Series

Somebody Else's Boy
The Gift of Christmas Yet to Come

Fabrian Books' Feel-Good Novels

A Holly Bay Christmas
A Highland Practice
The Christmas Shop at Central Park

The Channel View Farm Series

Give Me Your Answer Do
Second Chances at Channel View Farm

So Vain Books

Among A Thousand Stars

For Anna and Harry

The path through life might not always be smooth, but I know you'll find your song and someone to sing it with. All my love, Mum xx

Chapter One

By the time Anna emerged from the coffee shop, clutching a family-sized cup of caffeine that was her only hope of getting through the afternoon's meetings, the sky had turned iron grey. It felt dark enough to be going straight home, rather than heading back to the office after a snatched lunchbreak. No such luck. Even the twenty minutes she'd been out for was pushing it, and every moment of break she had during the day would just be added on to the end. There were no shortcuts working for Grayson, Hamilton and Jones, and just lately, living the dream didn't feel like living, at all.

The first drop of rain plopped onto the plastic lid of the coffee cup, sliding down the side, where the barista had scrawled her name. Kind of, anyway. He'd written Hannah instead of Anna. Not that it mattered—she was just another customer to him, an anonymous face in the crowd. Even if he'd got it right, he'd never have remembered it next time. When she'd first arrived in London, she'd liked that about the city, but being anonymous could lose its appeal.

Anna was almost running by the time she was halfway across Blackfriars' Bridge. Not because she wanted to—there was no point trying to outrun the rain—but everyone around her seemed to think they could beat the storm, and she just got dragged along with them. She pulled the hood of her jacket up to stop her carefully-straightened hair turning into the tangled disaster it would be if it got wet.

It was the second week of November, and the Christmas lights had been switched on the week before, but the festive spirit clearly hadn't arrived yet. People were jostling her on the pavement, and she nearly lost her coffee cup, dodging the prongs of an oversized golfing umbrella, which a man heading in the opposite direction seemed to be using to clear his path.

She'd almost be glad to get back to the office. *Almost*. Reaching the other side of the bridge, the crowd thinned out, scattering off in different directions, back to the offices and shops that would shelter them from the rain. Windows in the buildings around her glowed with artificial light, as the sky grew blacker and the rain seemed to double its pace. It was not a good time to be caught outside.

"Oi!"

The shout in front of Anna made her jump, and at first, she couldn't see where it had come from. Then, looking down, she spotted him.

A young guy, with a rough, matted beard, sat on some water-logged cardboard in front of the large recycling bins, just outside her office block. His beanie hat had been pulled down as low as it could be, and the rain dripped down off it, onto the already sodden sleeping bag at his feet - people trampling over it as if he wasn't even there.

"Are you okay?" She drew the sleeping bag towards him to try and stop anyone else treading on it, since he seemed to have given up. When he looked up at her, she couldn't be sure whether it was rain, or tears, making his face so wet. Either way, she wanted to cry, just looking at him.

"Is that a serious question?" He had a lovely, lilting West Country accent that took her by surprise. Although, she wasn't sure why.

"Erm, yes." Heat rose up Anna's neck, despite the drop in temperature that had accompanied the storm. "I mean, I know you're soaking wet and ..."

"Huddled by some bins in the pouring rain, with all my worldly possessions in a rucksack, and what passes for my bed floating in a puddle?"

"Well, yes, apart from that."

He didn't sound bitter, and when he smiled, Anna couldn't help smiling back. It was easy to forget that homeless people were just that: people. Maybe it was seeing them so frequently on the streets—over time, they just blended into the background—whilst she worried about deadlines and making enough of a return on her latest marketing campaign.

"I'm better, just for you asking."

"Do you like coffee?"

"Are you asking me out on a date?" He laughed, and she couldn't help wondering how he'd ended up on the streets, but she'd never make her meeting if she got into that.

"I just thought you might like my coffee. I haven't drunk out of it, yet, so it's perfectly safe."

"Do you know what? You've made me smile more in the last five minutes than I can remember in a long time. Not just stopping to check that I was okay and offering me your coffee, but for thinking I'd be worried about catching a cold from drinking out of your cup. You're a funny girl ..." He looked down at the side of the cup, as she passed it to him. "Hannah."

"It's Anna, actually, not that it matters. What's your name?"

"Dane. Pleased to meet you, Anna." He held out his hand, and she took it, trying not to imagine how long it might've been since he'd last had a wash. Guilt washing over her for even thinking it.

"I can't stop, because I'm late for a meeting, but I want you to take this." Reaching into her bag, she pulled five twenty-pound notes out of her purse. She was supposed to be paying two-hundred pounds towards a spa weekend that one of the secretaries was organising, but what the hell. She didn't want to go, anyway, and paying the deposit could definitely wait. Dane needed the money far more. "Maybe it'll be enough for you to get a hotel room for tonight, so you can get your stuff dry. It looks like the bad weather's set to last."

"Thank you, Anna." He turned the money over in his hand and looked up at her. "There's not many like you around, willing to give up so much for a stranger."

She smiled in answer, swallowing the lump in her throat. He had no idea she earned a hundred pounds an hour, and spent far too much of it on tall skinny lattes and weekend breaks she didn't want. A hundred pounds had come to mean almost nothing to her, and when it meant *so* much to someone like Dane, there was something seriously wrong in the world.

****

There was a queue for the lift up to the third floor of the office block, where Grayson, Hamilton and Jones had a suite of offices, so Anna decided to take the stairs. Hers was the smallest of the offices that had a view of the Thames, but it had still thrilled her to move in there with her most recent promotion, and to post pictures on Instagram and Facebook, showing the world just how far she'd come.

Her mother, Louise, who had no clue how to use Instagram, but seemed to be on Facebook every spare moment she had, must have shared the pictures with everyone she knew, as well as quite a lot of people she didn't. She wasn't averse to accepting friend requests from strangers, so much so, she'd almost had her laptop confiscated by Anna when she'd excitedly reported making friends with a Nigerian 'prince', who she'd been chatting to online. She'd been really put out when Anna had suggested he might be looking for a fake romance with a vulnerable woman, who'd be easily conned into parting with her cash. Especially as Anna's dad had been perched on the other end of the sofa the whole time she'd been messaging her new *friend*, and Louise had been desperate to announce at the next church coffee morning that she had royal connections. It must have been a big disappointment for a woman who seemed to have spent most of her life judging her worth by what other people thought. But social media was fatal for that, and Anna was no better in some ways. She hadn't told any of her four-hundred, or so, Facebook 'friends' how miserable she'd been in her job lately. No-one wanted to know the truth anyway.

Taking the stairs two at time, for the first two flights, Anna had to pause on the second floor to catch her breath. Pulling her mobile out of her bag, she found a message waiting.

✉ *Incoming message from Seb*
Hi Gorgeous. Got to have drinks tonight with the new clients from Saudi. Nigel has told me I need to show them a good time, so I'll have to take a rain check on dinner. Unless you want to help me with the entertaining, of course! Xx

She should have been disappointed that Seb had cancelled their dinner plans, but she wasn't. He was a nice enough guy—certainly a lot nicer than some of the others at the firm—but Anna had only drifted into a relationship with him because they spent so much time at the office together. All they talked about, whenever they went out, was work, anyway, and there was a danger it was all she'd have to talk about with anyone, if things carried on the way they were.

✉ *Outgoing message to Seb*
No worries. Nigel will probably have me working late, anyway, especially as I dared to have a lunch hour. Well, more twenty minutes than an hour, but you know it won't be looked upon favourably! Have fun entertaining, and we'll catch up for a chat soon X

She put a kiss at the end of the text, because everyone seemed to do it. It would have provoked a reaction if she'd suddenly stopped and, instead, added the line to the text that she wanted to: *we need to talk.* She didn't want him to think she was upset about the cancelled plans, but in that instant she'd made up her mind—at the bottom of the stairwell to floor three—she was going to tell him they'd be better off as friends.

At almost forty, Seb was ten years older than Anna, and he'd recently started making jokes about finding a wife. The last time they'd been out, he'd even hinted about giving her a diamond for Christmas. With December fast approaching, the last thing Anna wanted was a proposal. It wouldn't even be because Seb was head over heels in love with her, but because it was easier than finding someone else, when work took up so much of his time.

They both deserved more than that.

Opening the doors into the reception area of Grayson, Hamilton and Jones, she almost walked straight into the decorator.

Perched at the top of a large white step ladder, he was stringing fairy-lights onto the huge Christmas tree, which had been completely bare when she'd left for her coffee. Below him, two other members of his team shouted instructions and moved the tree millimetres to the left and right, searching for the perfect angle.

Another team of decorators were working in a cradle on the outside of the building, positioning a wreath with a diameter of at least twelve feet against the glass, the lashing rain apparently not a good enough reason to wait. It seemed Nigel Grayson was going all out this year, to prove that his corporate legal firm were doing better than ever–if you didn't count the wellbeing of his staff, at least.

"Anna, I'm so glad I caught you!" Stephanie Hayes, the junior partner whose secretary was organising the spa weekend, caught hold of her arm, as she walked past the tree. "Nina tells me you haven't paid your deposit yet, and I was wondering if you still wanted to go?"

"Well, I ..." Maybe she'd got Stephanie wrong, if she had enough insight to realise Anna was only going because she felt cornered.

"It's just that Mr Grayson's wife said she might like to join us, and the hotel haven't got another room available, so ..."

"So, it would suit you, if I didn't fancy it?" She couldn't help smiling—there were no surprises, after all. Stephanie knew that a weekend networking with the boss's wife would do far more for her career than a weekend with the Marketing Director. Still, it suited Anna, so why make Stephanie suffer the agony of denying what was blatantly obvious? "That's fine. I was struggling to make the time, anyway, so please let Fiona have my place."

She just hoped it would be as easy finishing things with Seb. She'd text him after work and arrange to meet up later in the week. She might as well do it whilst she was on a roll. If she didn't get a shift on and make the meeting with Nigel on time, though, it would be her head that would be rolling.

Rob, Nigel's P.A., glanced up, as she walked into the outer office, where his desk was situated, allowing him to guard access to the senior partner of the firm. "Get caught in that rain, did you?" He smiled. "Are you going into Mr Grayson's office like that, or do you want me to keep your jacket out here?"

"I'd forgotten I was still wearing it. Thank you." She returned Rob's smile. He was one of the nicest people at the firm, and no-one, least of all Anna, envied him his job. Staff at his level had to call Nigel 'Mr Grayson'—a man who was nothing, if not demanding. Being his personal assistant must have been a pretty thankless task.

"No problem, and you haven't forgotten about keeping an eye out for a flat for me, have you? Now that I've got the inheritance from my uncle, I can actually afford to live up here for a bit."

"I promise, I'll keep asking my landlord if anything comes up to rent, but he's already said he'll give you first refusal." She smiled again. "Just don't let me down. You know he's only doing it on my recommendation. So, no having wild parties every night of the week!"

"As if I'd have the energy after a day in this place."

She couldn't argue with that. Hanging up her jacket on the stand outside Nigel's office, she knocked on the door and waited to be summoned in.

"Enter," His deep voice boomed out and she checked her watch, before she opened the door. She definitely wasn't late, and only two minutes early, so that couldn't give him much to complain about.

"Good afternoon, Nigel." She'd been allowed to call him that since her most recent promotion and subsequent office move, four doors down from his.

"Is it? It looks pretty grim to me!" He laughed, and for a moment she could almost believe he had a sense of humour. "I bet those decorators putting up the wreath wish they'd worked a bit harder at school."

"I'm sure their job has its rewards." What could she say to someone who only saw money as a reward? He'd never understand that a decorator might have ten times more passion for their work than he did himself. Even if they were just doing it to put food on the table, they'd be doing it for people they cared about. She wondered if her boss could say the same.

"Let's get on then, shall we? First thing on the agenda are the Christmas hampers. What did your department go for in the end?"

"Fortnum and Mason Expeditions hampers for the directors of our most valued clients."

"How much?"

"A thousand pounds each." She tried not to think about Dane and his soaking wet sleeping bag, as she listed the clients her assistant had ordered hampers for.

"What about the clients with less revenue?" Nigel narrowed his eyes. Everyone's value was strictly based on the income they brought into the firm, not how important the work was in representing them, or how good they were to work with.

"Fortnum and Mason's do a range of hampers, right down to one that's only fifty-five pounds. My team have ordered some of those for individual staff within some of our client companies, too."

"As long as they're key staff and it breeds goodwill for more business."

"Of course." Anna swallowed. "And what about our own staff? Would you like my team to order some hampers for them?"

"They'd rather have the money!" Nigel laughed even louder, as if she'd suggested buying the staff a chocolate selection box, rather than a hamper filled with mulled wine, whisky infused fruit cake and clotted cream fudge. "I know I've got a reputation for making my staff work hard, but people know what they're getting into when they work for me. I'm not stupid. I'm fully aware they only work the long hours they do for the money they can earn."

"Of course, Christmas bonuses are what a lot of people rely on, but I thought perhaps a bit more of a personal thank you might be appreciated, too. Especially for some of the support staff who aren't entitled to Christmas bonuses."

"Secretaries and cleaners, you mean?"

"Well, some of the personal assistants get bonuses, but the reception staff, and the cleaning and catering team, don't. Then there's the doorman downstairs, as well—he deserves a thank you."

"How much are we talking about?"

"There are twenty-seven staff, with the doorman, not entitled to cash bonuses. So for the cheapest hampers, it's just short of fifteen hundred pounds." Surely he wouldn't begrudge almost thirty staff a bit of Christmas cheer, for less than the cost of two hampers for corporate clients who already had more money than they knew what to do with?

"Is it tax deductible?"

"The finance team have said they can find a way of making it count."

"You know it's your team's job to focus on bringing in new revenue and keeping the clients we've already got happy, don't you? Not making sure that everyone in this place gets a pat on the back, whether they deserve it, or not."

"Happy staff are more likely to work hard to keep the customers happy, and everyone in the organisation has a role to play." She'd learnt over the years she'd been working for Nigel that he quite liked it when she answered him back. There was a fine line she had to be careful not to cross, though, and five minutes into their meeting, she'd already come pretty close.

"You've got a point, I suppose. But your team needs to liaise with HR to go through the performance reviews of all the staff involved, to check they deserve it."

"Absolutely."

"That's sorted, then. Now, much more importantly, we need to set up a series of meetings with Mackenzie Bretton."

Mackenzie Bretton were a firm of Anglo-French financiers, who would become a major client, if Grayson, Hamilton and Jones won the contract for their legal representation.

Anna looked down at her notes. "They're asking for an initial meeting on December first, but your schedule says you aren't free."

Nigel buzzed through to his PA. "Robert?"

"Yes, Mr Grayson?"

"Get in here and bring my schedule with you."

Anna tried not to flinch at the lack of niceties. She should have been used to it, after working with Nigel for so long—Rob almost certainly was.

"Anna says I'm not free on the afternoon of the first? What's in the diary?"

Rob scrolled through the calendar on the iPad he was holding. "It's Finty's violin recital."

"Oh, God." Nigel pulled a face. "Bloody awful things, and it sounds like a thousand cats being strangled when she practices at home. Is Fiona around then?"

Rob looked down at the diary again. "Yes, she's in the UK on the first, so she's in the diary as being able to attend."

"Take that out of my diary, then, and clear the afternoon for the Mackenzie Bretton meeting. When do they want the follow up?"

"On the fourteenth of December, in the afternoon, but your diary's got Xander's first nativity play scheduled in for then."

"Who the hell put all these things in my diary?"

"Mrs Grayson asked your nanny to liaise with me, to get them scheduled in."

"Oh, for God's sake. Don't either of those bloody women realise I haven't got time for all this nonsense?" Nigel looked at Anna for agreement, but she couldn't bring herself to nod. "Is Fiona around for that one?"

"According to your schedules, she's speaking at a conference in Chicago that week, and she's not flying back until the fifteenth." Rob shot a quick look at Anna, a mutual understanding passing between them, and she knew what Nigel would say, even before he said it.

"Well, the blasted nanny will be there, won't she? She can just record it for us, and then we can fast forward to Xander's bit, instead of sitting through hours of tedious singing and kids bursting into tears for no reason."

"I'll update the schedule and let your nanny know. Do you need me for anything else?"

"No, you can go." Nigel waved a dismissive hand at Rob and turned to Anna. "Do we need to discuss a strategy for this meeting?"

She managed to shake her head. But in the last five minutes she'd been hit by a realisation that was going to change her life, and she was struggling to find the words to answer him. "Let me put some thoughts together and get them across to you this afternoon. I don't want to take up too much of your time."

"Good, right. Well, off you go, then."

It was her turn to be on the receiving end of Nigel's dismissive wave. He was clearly as glad to get rid of her, as she was to go.

Rob handed Anna her jacket, as she shut the door of Nigel's office behind her. "Are you alright, you look like you've seen a ghost? All the colour's drained out of your face."

"I can't do this, anymore."

"Do what?"

"Work for someone like Nigel, who thinks his kids are just an inconvenience. There's not one Christmas event he'd prioritise with his family, over making an even bigger fortune than he's already got."

"I know, but you can't leave! It'll be even worse here, without you."

"Then, why don't you leave, too?"

"Because he pays me a lot more than I could get elsewhere, and I want to live in London. It's got everything I love." Rob shrugged his shoulders. He was always talking about the latest West End show he'd seen, or a new exhibition he wanted to visit. London was the perfect city for Rob, but he'd never had enough money to live right in the centre of things before.

"I'm going to need to have a word with my landlord, but if he's happy for you to take over the lease, you could move into my flat. It would help us both out. I won't have to give notice, and you'll get a flat in the perfect location, with a half-decent landlord."

"You'll have to give notice on your job, though." His reluctance to see her leave seemed to have disappeared at the mention of the flat.

"They'll put me straight on gardening leave, if I resign. There'll be too much risk of me trying to poach clients, if they let me stay on. Especially if I let Nigel think it's because I'm going to work for another firm."

"You'd do that?" Rob looked suitably impressed.

"If it means I can get out of here sooner, rather than later, I'd do almost anything. But there are a few things I need to do this afternoon first, so don't breathe a word to anyone, okay?"

"My lips are sealed."

Leaving Rob to contemplate his potential flat move, she made a mental list of the things she needed to do before she could hand Nigel her resignation. She wanted to make sure the order went in for the support staff hampers, speak to her team, and give her landlord a ring.

But first on her list was to go back downstairs and see if Dane was still outside. The least she could do was give him the other hundred pounds she'd taken out of the cashpoint for the deposit on the spa weekend.

Without knowing it, he'd turned her life upside down. As scary as the changes she was about to make seemed, she was sure they were for the better. She just hoped the most important people in her world would see it the same way.

Chapter Two

Jamie scribbled some more details in his notebook, before looking up at the couple sitting in front of him, flanked by three of their friends.

"So, you want to have the wedding ceremony first, and then have Charlie christened straight afterwards?"

"I know it's unconventional." Kate Harris, the bride-to-be, shot him a nervous smile as she spoke. "But we thought it would be a lovely way for us to mark the start of our lives together. With me adopting Charlie on my own, and Will having to go through the process after we got together, we thought this would be the perfect way of uniting our little family, once and for all. Getting married on the same day as we officially recognise Charlie's change of surname feels right."

"I think it's a lovely idea." Jamie returned her smile. "I just want to make sure I get all the details right, and the order you want things to run."

"Frankly, we're just glad you can fit us in, and that you're willing to try and corral Charlie into sitting still for long enough to actually get christened." Will, Kate's fiancé, headed after Charlie, as he hurtled back down the aisle for the third time, the little boy's best friend, Toby, in hot pursuit.

"I'm hoping that seeing Charlie going through the process might make Toby less likely to scream the church down when it's his turn," Nancy, one of the intended godparents, said. "I'm just glad you haven't got the tree decorated, yet—or, even in my present state, I'd have to chase him up the aisle, too. He loves Christmas trees." She rested a hand on her baby bump, the violet shadows under her eyes a telling sign of how exhausting it was, looking after a lively toddler whilst heavily pregnant.

"There's nothing Charlie, or Toby for that matter, can throw at me that I haven't seen before." Jamie couldn't help laughing at the two boys, who were weaving out of Will's grasp like a couple of rugby stars in the making. "The tree was a donation from my father's estate, which is great, but I could have done without him having it delivered this early. We can't start decorating it until the first Sunday of advent, but every child who comes in here asks me why it's so bare. Still, I'm trying to practice gratitude, even with my dad."

"I take it nothing much has changed, then?" Sara, one of the three godmothers, widened her eyes. She and Jamie had known each other since he was in his teens.

"You know my dad." He shrugged. "Even acts of generosity have to be on his terms. But I'm sure you don't want to hear about that." He turned to Nancy. "Did you want me to put a date in the diary for Toby's christening, too?"

"We want to make it a joint one with his little sister, when she arrives, so maybe a date in early spring? I might have managed to shift a tiny bit of the baby weight by then, instead of looking like a blimp in a sandwich bag, in every dress I wear. Our wedding was pretty low key, so we might as well go all out for the christening. And I'd like at least one photo of me with Jack that I don't have to turn to face the wall!"

"And Jack's the godfather, right?" Jamie was still trying to get to grips with who everyone was. Although he'd grown up in St Nicholas Bay, he'd spent a lot of the time at boarding school, and ten years earlier he'd left town for good. Or, at least, that's what he'd thought at the time. Returning to the Bay, as the newly appointed vicar, a lot had changed, although other things seemed frozen in time. His father's attitude, for one.

Sara's mum, Louise, was the cleaner at the church, and there was almost nothing she didn't know about life in the Bay, and even less that she didn't want to pass on to him. So he already knew Nancy was a teacher at the local college, and her husband, Jack, had been a widower when he moved to the Bay with his baby boy Toby. They'd since got married, and had a little sister for Toby on the way. He'd met Kate and Will when they'd first asked if he'd marry them, so he knew a bit about them, too. They'd told him they were old school friends, but they hadn't got together until after Kate had adopted Charlie, a little boy with Downs Syndrome, two Christmases before. Sara was the only one he'd known from the old days, though, and he'd dated her sister Anna in his teens.

He'd been concerned, when he first found out that Louise cleaned the church, and her husband, Gary, looked after the grounds and maintenance. Would they have forgiven him for hurting their daughter, by breaking every promise he'd ever made her? He needn't have worried. If they even remembered that fateful summer, it was obviously ancient history to them. He'd thought about Anna a lot over the years, but coming back to St Nicholas Bay had brought her to the forefront of his mind. Hearing that she was busy with her career, and almost never made it back, had been a weird mixture of disappointment and relief.

"Yes, Jack's the only godfather, bless him, with three godmothers elbowing him out of the way. But he's working tonight. At least, that's what he says!" Kate exchanged a smile with Nancy as she spoke. "I know that's a bit unconventional, too, but I just couldn't choose between Sara, Meg and Nancy, so I had to have them all."

"That's fine." Jamie smiled at the third godmother, Meg. She attended the church with her family most Sundays and looked like she was struggling not to intervene in Will's attempts to control the boys. She tutted a couple of times, and as Nancy and Kate exchanged another look, Jamie did his best to break the tension, "I don't think a child can ever have too many people who love them in their lives." He wished he'd had a small army of godmothers in his life when his mum had died. Things might have worked out differently, but then he might never have found his vocation, either. Maybe God really did work in mysterious ways.

"And you don't mind that we're not exactly, well, you know, regular churchgoers?" Kate's cheeks coloured slightly.

"Just as well, given how Charlie and Toby are behaving!" Meg was unable to hold herself back any longer and she stood up. "I think I better go and give Will a hand. He's the one who needs to sit here and take in the seriousness of all this."

"Meg just likes things to be organised. She doesn't mean anything by it, Nance," Kate looked embarrassed as she turned to her friend. "She's always been the organiser, hasn't she, Sara?"

"She has, but that doesn't excuse her being rude to Nancy. She doesn't know Meg like we do, but even I thought that was out of order."

"It's fine." Nancy shrugged. "I know Toby can be a handful, but he's always just so excited when he sees Charlie, and I love seeing the two of them together."

"Please don't worry about the boys. It's nice to hear the church filled with laughter, and there's nothing they can damage." Jamie had been thrown out of chapel at school for talking, or laughing, more times than he could remember, and he definitely didn't want to have the sort of church where people were afraid to bring their children.

"Sorry about that." Will slid back into his seat beside Kate. "Meg's taken over, and she's already got the boys in order. They're going to do some colouring, apparently."

"There are lots of sheets from the family services, and I'm sure she'll find something to interest Charlie and Toby." Jamie looked down at his notebook again. He had to go through the legal requirements of the wedding, and being in charge of everything was still pretty new to him. "I'll need to read the banns on three Sundays before the wedding. So, given that the wedding and christening are on the second Sunday of

December, and we're now in mid-November, that means I'll need to start next Sunday."

"Do we have to be here for that?" Will raised a questioning eyebrow and earned an elbow in the ribs from his bride-to-be.

"I think that's the least we can do." Kate rolled her eyes. "In fact, I'd like to do something to thank you for letting us have the wedding here at such short notice. Maybe helping with the decorating of the church for advent, or the chapel in the harbour for the memorial star service?"

"That would be lovely, but it's not a condition of having the wedding here. I'm not going to hold you to ransom, or ask you to run a stall at the bring-and-buy sale for the next four years." Jamie laughed at the look of relief that crossed Will's face. Much as he needed all the volunteers he could get—between the main church and the tiny chapel in the harbour he was also responsible for overseeing—he wasn't into blackmailing people to attend his services. "It's not compulsory for you to be in church for the reading of your banns, either, but I think it would be nice if you could. Lots of couples find it really meaningful, and they often feel more connected with the church as a result."

Kate grasped Will's hand. "Of course we'll be here."

Jamie glanced down at his notebook again. "What about flowers?"

"Sounds like I got here just in time!"

Louise, Sara's mother, marched down the aisle at a double quick pace at the mention of flowers. Jamie hadn't even heard her arrive. Although she was only responsible for keeping the church clean on a very part-time basis, Jamie had quickly realised that Louise liked to have a handle on everything that was going on.

"Does that mean you're volunteering to help out with the flowers, Lou?" Kate stood up and kissed the older woman on both cheeks.

"Of course! You're like a third daughter to me, and you know me, there's nothing I like more than a good wedding. Especially since neither of my girls have given me one." Louise took a seat next to her daughter without waiting to be invited.

Sara screwed up her face. "You do know I've been married for nearly twenty years, don't you, mum?"

"Yes, but a quickie service in a dingy registry office, when you were barely eighteen and with the twins already on the way, hardly counts as any mother's dream wedding for their daughter, does it?"

"Just as well you've got Anna, then, isn't it? I'm sure she won't disappoint. She's always done everything right." Sara turned her body slightly away from her mother, and Jamie cleared his throat. It was definitely time for another change of subject.

Thankfully, Kate thought so, too. "Can I come down and talk to you about the flowers in the week, Lou? I'm sure Mum will want to come, as well."

"That would be lovely and I've got some ideas already." Louise beamed at her. Either oblivious to how much she'd upset Sara, or choosing to ignore her. "I've got lots of ideas for decorating the church and the chapel for Christmas, too, Jamie. I thought we could have wreaths on the leaded windows, hung with big red ribbons. I think it would be too much on the stained glass, though. We don't want to end up looking tacky."

"Indeed." Jamie suppressed a smile. "Perhaps we can set up a meeting to discuss that next week?"

"Ooh, yes. I'll text you."

He just hoped he wouldn't end up regretting giving Louise his mobile number. She'd sent him at least ten texts in the past week alone, but she meant well. He'd just have to keep praying for more patience.

"Okay, well, that's sorted, then." Jamie looked at the group in front of him and felt a stab of envy—something else to continue to pray for help in overcoming, given it was one of the seven deadly sins. But he was only human, and he couldn't help wishing he had a group of friends like Kate and Will had.

He'd moved around too much over the past few years, and he doubted many of his friends from boarding school would have anything in common with him, anymore. Most of them were running family estates, or working in high-flying jobs in the city. As for friends in St Nicholas Bay itself, there'd never been too many of those. He'd played with some of the children of his father's staff when he'd been really young, but they'd mostly moved on quite quickly. No-one worked with his father for long. In the Bay itself, there'd only ever really been Anna, and he'd messed that up so spectacularly, he doubted she'd ever want to speak to him again. Some bridges just couldn't be rebuilt.

He forced his mind back to the present. "Is there anything else you wanted to cover this evening? We'll meet again before the big day, of course."

"No I think that's it, and thanks again, so much." Kate stood up at the same time as he did, and she leant forward to give him a hug, the smell of her perfume taking him back ten years and jolting his senses.

It was the same perfume Anna wore—at least the same perfume she'd worn back then. It was funny how a smell could evoke a whole host of memories.

"You're more than welcome, Kate, and it'll be an honour to officiate at the wedding and little Charlie's christening. Nice to meet you all, too." Jamie shook their hands, and one by one, everyone apart from Sara and Louise headed out of the church doors, into the inky blackness that had enveloped the churchyard in the time they'd been talking. The nights were drawing in fast, and it would be the shortest day before long. Christmas was just around the corner, too.

"Do you want me to give you a lift home?" Sara asked, as Louise fussed with straightening a pile of hymn books.

"No, your father's popping up any minute, to have a word with a vicar about some of the memorials left on the graves in the churchyard. There's one, or two, of them making weeding very tricky."

Jamie made another silent prayer for patience in response to Louise's words. Her husband, Gary, was just as well-meaning as she was, but they both seemed so set in their ways, so clear about what was right and what was wrong. As far as Jamie was concerned, people could do whatever they liked to make the graves of their loved ones special. If it gave them comfort, then it was okay by him, and he'd bet his last pound that God thought the same.

"Okay, then." Sara buttoned up her coat. "Are you and Dad coming to mine for lunch after you're finished here on Sunday?"

"I don't think we will this week, love. Anna's sent me a message, to say she's coming down and she's got some news for us." Louise was beaming again, the thought of her youngest daughter coming home clearly lifting her spirits. "I expect it's yet another promotion. We're so proud of her."

"Really, Mum, you've never mentioned that before." Sara's face clouded, and, despite the sarcasm, Jamie recognised the hurt in her eyes—he'd seen that same look in his own reflection all too often.

Having a father who thought his choice of career was laughable, Jamie could empathise with Sara feeling like second best. If he remembered rightly, she was eight, or nine, years older than Anna, and he was younger than his brother by a similar gap. But it seemed they had more than that in common.

"I'll see you when I see you, then, Mum," Sara said, "but I might text Anna and see if she wants to come on Sunday, too. Then she can give us all her big news at the same time."

Louise shrugged. "Whatever Anna thinks is best is fine by me and your dad."

"Don't I know it?" Sara muttered, closing the church door behind her and following her friends into the night—no doubt wishing she'd left with them.

Despite their agreement to discuss it later, Louise started talking to Jamie at twenty to the dozen about her plans for decorating the church for Christmas. Not that he was listening. All he could think about was that Anna would be back in St Nicholas Bay for the weekend and there was a chance he might bump into her. More than a chance, if he had his way. He wasn't sure whether the knot in his chest was excitement, or something else. He'd behaved like an idiot when he'd ended things between them, and she might still hate him as much as he'd hated himself back then. Either way, he had to find out. It had been ten years too long already.

Chapter Three

Hearing the rattle of the letterbox, Anna's fat ginger cat, George, briefly lifted his head from the warm pile of just-ironed clothes he'd settled down on.

There'd been more to pack than she'd anticipated, but luckily Rob was so thrilled to be taking on the flat that he'd said she could leave some of it, until she was settled elsewhere. There was no way it was going to fit in her room back at her parents' house, but staying there was going to be as temporary an arrangement as possible, anyway. If they even let her stay. Thankfully, her landlord had been more than happy for her to pass the tenancy straight over to Rob, since it saved him having to advertise and vet potential tenants.

The only moment of doubt she'd had about leaving her job was when she'd woken up in the night—two days after handing in her notice—from a vivid dream about telling her mum the news. It had felt so real, and Anna was under no illusion about how the news would be received—disappointment didn't come close. Her sister, Sara, would probably understand, but Anna had seen her be on the receiving end of their mum's disappointment often enough to know that it hurt.

At least everything else had seemed to fall into place. Nigel predictably hadn't taken the news well, and there'd been some fairly colourful language on his part. He'd called her an idealistic idiot, when she'd told him why she wanted to leave and that she wanted to do something that made a difference. When he'd realised he couldn't change her mind, he'd told her to clear her desk and get out. As she'd suspected, she was on gardening leave for the duration of her notice period, even though she hadn't lied in the end about having a new job. It meant she'd have three months where she'd be paid in lieu of notice, but couldn't start any paid work—pretty standard practice for a firm like Grayson, Hamilton and Jones, when senior staff moved on. A clause to protect themselves, so that Anna couldn't poach any of their clients. Nigel clearly wasn't convinced that she meant what she'd said about changing her career completely, and that she would much rather take a job on the checkout at Tesco than work for another corporate law firm, but she was glad. It meant she could go home to St Nicholas Bay straight away.

She'd always loved living there, but there was never any time as special as Christmas. Maybe it was inevitable in a town that had so many links to *A Christmas Carol*, which Dickens was rumoured to have partly-written whilst staying at an old coaching inn there. Whether it was true, or not, the town had embraced the legend, and lots of the shops were named after characters from the book, from the DIY store, *Marley's Chains*, to *Tiny Tim's Toys*.

Going home, at least initially, seemed the natural choice. She didn't have as many close links to the town as her sister did, of course. Sara had gone to school there, and had a close group of friends who all still lived in the Bay. She'd never left, having got married almost straight out of school, and then gone to work in the local primary school when the twins started there. Now that they'd hit their late teens, Sara had begun retraining as a midwife, and Anna was so proud of what she'd achieved.

Her niece and nephew were both heading off to university, to study for worthwhile careers. Liam wanted to be an occupational therapist, and Jade wanted to teach maths to secondary school pupils. Brave girl. Sadly, the disappointment that had been so evident from Anna and Sara's parents, when Sara had told them she was pregnant at eighteen, had never been erased, no matter what she did. But Anna had been thrilled to discover she was going to be an auntie, just at the same time she'd started at the grammar school in Canterbury, half an hour away from the Bay. Her mother had been far less thrilled to discover that she was going to be a grandma at forty-two, and had largely chosen to ignore it, after the initial furore. She'd spent the whole nine months talking about how well Anna was getting on, and how proud she was of her for getting into grammar school. It could have driven a wedge between Anna and Sara, but her sister had told her years later that Anna's excitement about being an auntie, and a bridesmaid at Sara and Joe's wedding, had made it so much easier to handle their parents' reaction. Sara's friends had been with her every step of the way, too.

Although Anna had made plenty of friends at school, they'd been spread out across the towns and villages around Canterbury, and there hadn't been that same close and enduring bond. She'd moved to London for university, and the three closest friends she'd made there had ended up spread across the globe: one in LA, one in New York, and the other one in Melbourne. Social media might have been good for keeping in touch, but it wasn't quite the same. Although it did come in handy when she woke up in the dead of night and needed someone to talk to.

She'd be starting over in the Bay, though. Hopefully, there'd be a new job as soon as her contract expired, a new flat, and the chance to build up a new group of friends. Work had got in the way of everything over the past few years, but the Christmas celebrations in the Bay would be the perfect time to put that right.

"Let's see what we've got, then, George"

The cat opened one eye as Anna spoke, but didn't bother to raise his head again, making the most of the last bit of warmth from the ironing pile, with his back resting against the radiator. He wasn't the most outdoorsy of cats in the summer, but in the winter, he only ever nipped out to do what a cat needed to do, and then he was straight back inside again, looking for the closest spot of warmth.

Anna flicked through the pile of post, wondering if she'd made a mistake in arranging to have it redirected when she moved. It was mostly junk mail and three Christmas catalogues amongst the day's delivery. Did she want to get her family matching tartan monogramed pyjamas? Not really. The family on the front of the catalogue looked happy enough about it, as they gathered around an open fire and passed each other beautifully-wrapped gifts. Anna just hoped her family would still be speaking to each other by Christmas day.

As for beautifully wrapped gifts, it wouldn't be Christmas, if her mum didn't buy Anna and Sara matching hat, glove and scarf sets. Anna had loved it when she was little—matching her big sister had seemed so cool—but it had far less appeal by the time she reached her teens. It had grown into a well-embedded family tradition, now, where she and Sara exchanged a secret smile. It meant their mother putting them on an equal footing for once, too.

"There's a Christmas card from your grandma, George."

Was it weird that she talked to her cat and, even worse, that she referred to her mother as George's grandma? If it was, it was tough. Rescuing George had been one of the best decisions she'd made since moving to London. She'd worried that a lifelong city cat might not enjoy country life, but as long as he had a radiator to curl up against, she was sure he'd be okay.

Her mother's neat handwriting would have been unmistakeable, even if she hadn't covered the envelope with stamps saying *'Direct from the North Pole'* and *'Santa stops here'*. Her mother had always loved Christmas, and it was inevitable that her card would be the first to arrive. Even sending one late-November was quite restrained for her. The Christmas tree might even be up already when Anna got home, unless her father had managed to win the battle they had every year and got her to agree that the first of December was the absolute earliest it would be sociably acceptable to decorate.

Either way, her mum would be desperate to break out the fairy-lights that lit up their house like the Blackpool illuminations, and had her dad making jokes about selling his kidney to pay the electricity bill in January.

Ripping the envelope right through the middle of a metallic snowman sticker, Anna pulled out the card and opened it to the message:

Merry Christmas Anna and a very happy new year. We're sure it will bring you so much success and we're prouder every year of our little high flyer. All our love Mum and Dad xx

Anna slid the card into the open suitcase on the bed and lifted George off the ironing pile. Meowing in protest, he hooked one claw into the back of her hand as a warning shot.

"Sorry, boy, but I've got to finish the packing. We've got a train to catch tonight."

He was going to be even less happy about being put into his pet carrier for the journey back to St Nicholas Bay. Sebastian had offered to drive her back, but she didn't want to use him, or make him think she might still change her mind about leaving London—and him—behind. Her mother had assumed she was just coming home for a weekend visit, and Anna hadn't done anything to shatter her illusions. It wasn't a conversation she wanted to have over the phone.

It wasn't a conversation she *wanted* to have, at all.

Packing the absolute essentials in her suitcase, she tried wheeling it down the corridor of the flat, with her laptop and handbag both strapped diagonally across her chest and the empty pet carrier in her hand. She was getting a cab to London Bridge station, and her dad would be picking her up at the other end, so she should just about be able to manage it. Even with George adding considerable weight to the equation.

When the doorbell rang, she almost tripped over one corner of the suitcase. It couldn't be the cab already.

Pressing the button on the intercom, she glanced at her watch. She still had fifteen minutes until it was due to arrive. "Hello."

"Anna, it's me." Seb's cut-glass voice was instantly recognisable, like the slump in her shoulders when she heard it.

She didn't want this. A clean get away: that was the plan.

"I've ordered a cab, Sebastian." She used the long version of his name, determined to keep the distance between them. "It'll be here any minute."

"Please let me take you."

"It's too late to cancel the cab now."

"At least let me come up and say goodbye properly."

"We've already done that." She sighed, but pressed the buzzer to let him up, anyway. Too guilty about the thought of him standing out on the street, begging to come in, to say no. It was just as well she was going, or she might've found herself persuaded to continue a relationship her heart wasn't in, either. "You can come up, but you've literally got two minutes. I've got to be ready to go in ten."

Unhooking her handbag and laptop, she propped them up against the suitcase in the hallway. It might make it tight for Seb to squeeze past, but it should leave him in no doubt that she meant what she'd said.

"You're really going, then?" His eyebrows disappeared beneath his perfectly blow-dried fringe, as he stepped into the hallway, as if he'd expected her impending departure to be some sort of ploy for attention. Was it really so difficult to believe that she didn't want this life anymore?

"Yes, like I said, in about ten minutes."

"And you've actually given up the tenancy on this place—you're not just sub-letting it? Don't you think that was a bit hasty?"

"I'm not coming back, so why would I want to do that?"

"Don't get me wrong." Seb gave her a knowing look, and his voice took on that slightly patronising tone that had always made her wonder if he thought he was better than her. "I can see the appeal of country life, that whole looking back at childhood with rose-coloured spectacles. Sometimes, I long for the Berkshire countryside. But when you get down to Kent, I give it a week before you're missing all of this."

"I need a fresh start."

"Running back to the place where you grew up is hardly a fresh start." A slight note of annoyance overtook his patronising tone.

She still liked Seb, a lot more than she'd ever liked Nigel, but in some ways, he had the same attitude. Everyone should come round to his way of thinking, and when they didn't, his patience didn't last long. Maybe it came with their training—lawyers argued for a living, after all.

"It's a starting point. I might stay, I might not. But I can't stay here, and I want to be back in St Nicholas Bay for Christmas." Maybe he was right about rose-coloured spectacles, but she wanted to throw herself back into small town life for the festive season. The parade and the tree lighting, the nativity service in the church, the pantomime in the old village hall, the Dickens' Christmas market, and drinking mulled wine whilst she watched the carol service at the memorial tree lighting in the harbour—all of it. Where the next year took her would be anyone's guess, but Christmas was definitely taking her home.

"Maybe I could come and see you. I'm taking almost a week off over Christmas."

"Good for you, but I don't think coming to see me would be a good idea." Anna had never wanted to hurt him, but it had to stop. What they'd had had been convenient—no great passion on either side—and it had already drifted along for much longer than it should have done.

"There's someone else, isn't there?"

"Yes."

"I knew it, who is he?" As tempting as it was to pretend he was right, and even though it would probably make life easier, she couldn't do it.

"It's not a he, it's me. I'm the someone else."

"I don't understand you, Anna. We could have had something."

"If you think that, Seb, then you're right. You don't understand me." She scooped up George as she spoke and put him in the cat carrier, shutting the door before he had a chance to escape. "But I don't think you understand yourself, either. Take that time off, take longer if you can, and think about what you really want. You'll soon realise it's not me."

"You're wrong." Seb shook his head, and when the doorbell buzzed again, Anna could have kissed the cab driver for being ten minutes early.

"I hope Christmas makes your wishes come true, and I know this time next year, you'll be thanking me for ending things between us when I did." She reached up, pecked Seb on the cheek, and virtually pushed him out of the door. Sometimes, you had to be cruel to be kind, and she was certain Seb would realise she was right before long.

If only she could say the same about her parents.

Chapter Four

"Sara! I didn't expect to see you here. Aren't you supposed to be at uni?" Anna put George's pet carrier down and threw her arms around her sister. The cat had meowed loudly for the first half hour of the journey, but his snoring had been almost as loud as that since, and he seemed to have complained himself out.

"I don't have any lectures on a Friday, so when I'm not on placement, I get the day off." Sara hugged her. "I hope it's not a disappointment."

"Of course it isn't. It's so lovely to see you, and it's a relief not to have to travel back with Dad and have him asking how work's going and what my big news is. Maybe I should just have kept my mouth shut about that, but I was worried I'd bottle out altogether, if I didn't put it out there."

"Are you pregnant?" Sara's eyes widened, and she ran a hand through her hair.

"No!" Anna laughed. Maybe it could've been worse, after all. "But I've quit my job."

"What? Oh, my God, how are you going to manage? And what's Mum going to say!" Sara's words came out in the same sort of rush as the thoughts that ran through Anna's head, whenever she thought about telling her mum.

"The managing bit is easy. I'm on three-months' gardening leave, on full pay, and I've got a bit of a nest egg put by. At least enough that I've got the time to make the right decision about what to do next. As for what mum's going to say, I think we both know that isn't going to be pretty."

"Do you know she put a picture of the view from your new office on the mantelpiece?" Sara laughed, but it didn't quite reach her eyes. "She even shoved the picture of the twins that had been in that spot right along to the end."

"I'm sorry." Anna hugged her sister again. If anything worthwhile came from disappointing her mother, it might make her realise what amazing things Sara had done with her life. Anna envied her. She had a happy marriage to a man who adored her, two kids who were coming out of the other side of teenage angst and finally learning to appreciate what a great mum she was, a close circle of friends, and a rewarding new career in the making. Sara was the one her mum should be telling everyone about.

"It's not your fault. It never has been." Sarah took the handle of Anna's case, so she could pick up the pet carrier. "Let's get in the car before the weather turns, and you can tell me why you left."

Above them, the sky was turning threateningly dark. It felt too cold to just be rain on the way, but it was too early for snow. White Christmases were the stuff of Hallmark greeting cards and made-for-TV movies. Snow almost always never arrived in the Bay until January—if at all.

With George settled in the back of the car and the seat belt securing his carrier in place, they set off towards their parents' house. Anna's stomach was churning. She hadn't felt so nervous since picking up her exam results as a teenager, and praying that they'd meet her mum's expectations. She couldn't remember ever being pleased for herself. She'd just wanted to please her mum. It had taken the best part of thirty years to start to break that cycle, and it was going to be a big adjustment for them all.

Sara didn't slow down, on the short journey to their parents' house on the edge of town, even as the road out of St Nicholas Bay became windier. If Anna hadn't had George and a heavy suitcase, it would have been perfectly walkable. They went along the road by the harbour, where a group of men were unloading a huge Christmas tree, ready for the illumination ceremony that always took place on the first weekend of

December. She'd missed it over the last few years, but she wanted to immerse herself in the full St Nicholas Bay experience this time around.

Besides, she might need a reason to get out of the house.

"So, come on, then, spill it. Did something happen with Sebastian that made you quit your job?" Sara asked.

"It had nothing to do with Seb. Although, I was getting worried that he was building up to a big proposal that neither of us *really* wanted. I left because it's all so meaningless. I want to do something worthwhile."

"Doing something worthwhile doesn't often lead to a six figure salary."

"And the old saying that money doesn't buy you happiness is true, too."

"Have you got *any* idea what you want to do?"

"I think I'd like to work for a charity." Anna suddenly pictured Dane, the homeless man she'd given the money to on the day she'd decided to quit. Helping people like him would feel worthwhile.

"Well, I think it's great." Sara pulled up outside the immaculate end-of-terrace house that they'd both grown up in. "But it's time to face the music. Are you going to do it straight away?"

"I might as well." Anna carried George into the house, as Sara insisted on taking her suitcase. She'd always been the big sister, treating Anna as if she needed looking after, even now they were both grown women.

"Anna banana, it's so good to see you." Her dad pulled her into his arms for such a powerful hug that she barely kept hold of George's pet carrier. He smelt reassuringly of the Old Spice aftershave he'd always worn.

"You, too, Dad. I'm just going to let George out in the back garden, and then I can tell you my news. Where's Mum?"

"She's on her way back from the church. We've got some exciting news about that, too, actually. But your mum will kill me, if I let on before she gets back. That's if Sara hasn't already told you?"

Sara shook her head, and Anna wondered what exciting news there could possibly be about the church where her mum had cleaned for years, and her dad had started doing maintenance and gardening when he'd left the local council. Maybe they had a new stained glass window, or a celebrity was getting married there. A few well-known names had started to move into the area over the last decade. Most of them were based in London, but had holiday homes in the Bay. It didn't go down well with the locals, but one of them having their wedding in the pretty little church where her own parents had got married would definitely count as big news in the town.

Letting George out of his pet carrier in the back garden, she watched him get accustomed to his new surroundings. He stretched out his front legs, then arched his back, before padding across to the patio, finding the only patch of warmth by the tumble drier outlet, and lying down again. He really was the world's laziest cat.

"Anna!" Her mother nearly knocked her flying. Her blonde hair was streaked with grey these days, but it was pulled neatly into a chignon, just as it had been for as long as Anna could remember, and even after a day's cleaning, there wasn't a hair out of place. She smelled of lemons, with a faint hint of bleach, but that had nothing to do with Anna's stomach lurching again. She'd never envied George and his carefree lifestyle more. "I couldn't wait to get home from the church and see you. I've been dying to hear your news, and I've been trying to guess what it is all week. I told the girls at the WI that it's bound to be big, if it warrants a trip home!"

"I want to hear all about the big news at the church first." It was only putting off the inevitable, but it would keep the smile on her mum's face for five more minutes. "Shall I put the kettle on?"

"I'll do it, love. You grab George and bring him inside, and then you can tell the three of us together. You don't want to leave him outside by himself until he's got the knack of knowing when to get out of the seagulls' way."

Anna picked up the ginger cat, who purred happily as he draped himself across one of her shoulders. He was getting really heavy. She'd fed him up after rescuing him, but a new life in the country should hopefully mean more exercise for him. Either that, or he'd have to cut back on the tuna he'd grown so partial to.

Her mother already had the tea service set out, and she was piling biscuits on a plate—custard creams and bourbon biscuits, the stuff of childhood that Anna only ever ate when she was at home with them.

"So, what's going on at church that's so exciting?" Anna warmed her hands on the cup of tea Sara had poured out. George was curled up on her lap, already sleeping again. Lucky thing.

"There's a new vicar at the church, and you'll never guess who it is!" Her mum's eyes shone with excitement.

"I don't know, one of the vicars who does *Pause for Thought* on Radio Two?" Anna couldn't have named any of them for a million pounds, but she knew her mum was an avid listener.

Louise shook her head. "No, guess again!"

"Someone from *Songs of Praise*?"

As her mother shook her head again, Anna racked her brains for somebody else who could possibly be the new vicar.

"Oh, I know. That lady vicar who used to be on *Gogglebox*!"

"No, still not even warm."

"I think you're right, then, Mum. I really never will guess—or, at least, not until your tea's gone stone cold. I think you're going to have to tell me."

"It's Jamie!"

"Jamie who?" Anna looked at Sara, who gave her a half-nod.

There'd only ever been one Jamie in Anna's life, but one of those had been more than enough, and there was absolutely no way it could be him. Sara's reaction must have been involuntary.

"Jamie Harrington, of course!" Her mother looked delighted, and every time she spoke, the pitch of her voice rose a little bit more. Anna's face must have gone as blank as her mind, since her mother felt the need to prompt her further. "Don't tell me you've forgotten Jamie. You two used to be so close, once upon a time. You know Jamie, Lord Harrington's younger son."

"I know who you mean, Mum. I'm just struggling to get my head around the idea that Jamie's a vicar. Let alone that he's back in St Nicholas Bay."

"I couldn't believe it, either." Sara gave her a sympathetic smile, clearly aware that Anna didn't share their mother's excitement at the news.

Her big sister had been the only person who'd known the full extent of Anna's broken heart, when Jamie had suddenly just disappeared from her life, almost without a word, and totally out of the blue, as far as she was concerned. Maybe coming back to St Nicholas Bay would turn out to be a mistake, after all. If her parents overreacted to her news, and the only person who'd ever broken her heart was going to pop up around every corner, she wasn't sure if she could make it to the other side of Christmas. Jamie was probably happily married by now, too. He might even have children happily living up at the vicarage—that was something she could believe. But Jamie as a vicar? It still didn't make any sense.

"Well, you better both believe it, because he is, and he's doing a marvellous job. He's like a breath of fresh air, after Reverend Johns. God bless him, but he was so doddery in the end that he was falling asleep in his own sermons." Louise laughed and filled up the teacups again. "So, come on, then. What's your big news?"

Still reeling from the discovery that Jamie was back, Anna just blurted it out, with none of the careful preamble she'd rehearsed in her head on the train coming down. "I've left my job."

"Really?" Her mother put her tea cup down with a clatter. "So, where are you going to, instead? You didn't say you've been applying for other jobs, let alone going for interviews."

"I haven't."

"So, have you been headhunted?" The excitement was back in Louise's voice, and Anna shook her head slowly.

"No, I just quit. I've come home while I'm working out my notice. I'm not allowed to go into the office, in case I try and steal their clients, but they're still paying me, and I can't start a new job until February."

"Why would you just quit?" her father chipped in. "Did something happen with Seb?"

Her mother seemed to have lost the power of speech. She opened and closed her mouth, like a fish out of water desperate to be thrown back in.

"Why does everyone think it's got something to do with Seb? None of you even met him!"

"What do you mean *everyone*?" Louise said, suddenly finding her voice again. "I suppose Sara knew already. Did she influence you?"

"Don't you dare!" Anna put George down on the floor and stood up. Enough was enough. She refused to listen to her mother putting Sara down, any more than she was prepared to tolerate Nigel side-lining his kids as an inconvenience. "I told Sara on the way from the station. That's when she found out about it. But maybe I should have told her how I was feeling sooner, how I've been feeling about the job, and how empty it's left me for months—maybe even *years*. Because Sara would have listened to me, and not thought about how my leaving the job would affect her. I've been miserable, Mum. And Seb made me miserable, too, and to be honest, I don't think I did much more for him, either. So, you haven't got a daughter who's a director anymore, or who might just get engaged to a hotshot lawyer. But what I hope you'll have, by the time Christmas is over, is a daughter who's happy again. If I can end up half the person Sara is, then I'll be prouder of myself than I've ever been." She turned away—she didn't want to hear their reaction—even as her mother started to protest.

Sara laid a hand on her arm. "Anna, don't go."

"I think we all need time to process this." Her father put a comforting arm around her mother, as he spoke, and Anna nodded her head.

That was their way—avoiding facing emotions head-on—and for once, it suited Anna just fine.

****

Outside, the late November air had grown cooler, making Anna wish she'd stopped to grab a coat. Walking briskly might warm her up a bit, though, so she set off at a pace towards the town.

Most of the trees she passed were already bare, but there were still one, or two, split conker shells amongst the leaves littering the edge of pavement, the shiny conkers long since collected by local children. There was no plan for where she was heading, but she stopped by the parish noticeboard to read a flyer about the Christmas parade. Maybe she should volunteer to help out? She read to the bottom, and was about to take down the contact number of one of the organisers, when she saw it: *Reverend Jamie Harrington.* It was like seeing Prime Minister Santa Claus, or Archbishop Easter Bunny written down. His name up there seemed just as ridiculous.

"Will you be volunteering?"

Even before she turned around, she recognised the voice. Hit by an overwhelming feeling of fight, or flight, but deciding there'd already been enough drama for one day, she turned around to face him.

She'd told her mother what she thought about the way she'd treated Sara, so it should've been easy enough to tell the man who'd dumped her as a teenager why she'd rather go back to working for Nigel than volunteer for anything he was involved with.

"It's so lovely to see you, Anna." He pulled her into a hug, before she managed to utter a word.

He smelt of sandalwood and sea air. She didn't want him to make her feel safe and protected, like he'd done all those years before, but somehow he did. When she'd been in Jamie's arms, it had always felt like everything was going to be okay. Maybe it was his height, at well over six feet tall, or that rugby player's physique, which had sent the boys who'd followed her home from the bus stop scattering in all directions, the first time they'd met. His hair was still the colour of wet sand on the beach, where'd they walked a hundred times just to be together. She wanted to hate him for leaving her, but in truth she never really had. The anger that had boiled over so many times in the early days, and that she'd fantasised about confronting him with, seemed to still, the moment he put his arms around her again. Maybe it was seeing a friendly face in the wake of her parents' obvious disappointment, but whatever it was, she was happy to see him.

"You look exactly the same." Jamie took a step back and she noticed his dog collar for the first time, but it still just looked like he was dressing up.

She tucked a strand of dark hair behind her ear and pulled herself up to her full five-feet-four. "I've grown at least two inches since we last met, so you can't call me short-arse anymore."

"I wouldn't dream of it." He laughed, and she felt silly, acting like the teenager she'd been when he'd left. "For the record, you look fantastic. You always did."

"I still can't believe you're a vicar." She hadn't meant to just come out with it, but standing there, looking at him, nothing was going according to plan.

"I get that a lot." He paused when she shivered and took off his coat. "Here, take this. You look half-frozen, and I've just walked up the cliff path from the beach, so I was too hot, anyway.

A big part of her wanted to say no, but an even bigger part of her wanted the warmth—not just of the coat, but the gesture. Hadn't she said she needed to make friends back in the Bay? That was all she was doing—being friendly, just like Jamie—and it would have been churlish to say no.

"Thank you." She pulled the coat on. It was ridiculously big on her, but already warm, and there was a subtle trace of sandalwood on the collar. "So, you're going to need to explain this to me, the whole vicar thing. I just can't get my head around it. You never seemed the type, not in a million years."

"What's the type?"

"Not you!"

"Fair enough." He laughed that easy laugh of his again, which had always made her smile, even when they'd been having one of the petty falling outs they'd had so often as teenagers. "I don't know. Call it a flash of inspiration, a moment of clarity, but when it came, I just knew it was what I wanted to do. I suppose *had to do* would be more accurate."

"So, is that why you left?"

"No." Jamie met her gaze for a moment. She'd forgotten just how blue his eyes were. "I left to get away from Dad, and all the things he wanted me to be that I didn't want. One day, it all just got too much. I'm sorry, though. I should have told you. But I've never been great at saying goodbyes, especially when you were the one person I didn't want to say goodbye to."

"It's all ancient history now." It was strange, but she meant it. She'd almost forgotten how close they'd grown, and so quickly, partly because of the shared experience of overbearing parents and the desire they'd both had to escape the Bay as a result. Funny how they'd ended up coming back at more, or less, the same time.

"It means a lot that you can forgive me. Although, I'm still not sure that I can forgive myself."

"You don't need to keep punishing yourself on my account. Did you start your training as soon as you left?"

"I went out to India, backpacking, like we always said we would." They exchanged another look. "I started working in an orphanage out there, and the feeling of wanting to serve God crept up on me. There was so much tragedy, so much suffering, and yet, amongst it, there was this group of people sacrificing their time to do good for others. They were volunteers from a Christian centre, and when I watched them working, it was as if I could see the meaning in life for the first time. It felt like my calling, and when I got back to the UK, I started the process of training to become a vicar. I worked two jobs to fund my degree in theology and pastoral studies, and I completed the last stage of my training earlier this year. My intention was always to go back out to India, or Africa, or somewhere I felt my help was really needed. But then the vacancy at St Nicholas Bay came up, and it felt like another calling. A chance to lay some ghosts to rest, to try and rebuild a relationship with my father and brother, and do something for the parish that might put right some of my wrongs in the past."

"Wow. So, India really was a life changing experience." It was going to sound mundane in comparison, to say that her moment of clarity had happened just over Blackfriars' Bridge—especially when they'd planned to see India together. They'd both just finished their A-levels, and had talked about taking a gap year together, but then he'd just gone without her. She didn't want to rake it up, though. What was the point? They'd both moved on, but maybe her life would have changed as much as his had, if she'd gone with him. Or maybe it would always have taken seeing Dane—sitting on a soaking wet sleeping bag as the world rushed by—to really change her views.

"It was, but I did wish you were there."

"Like I said, it's all in the past." She squeezed her eyes shut for a second, blaming the sharp wind coming off the sea for the stinging in her eyes.

"So, what about you? Your mum tells me you're a highflyer in the city."

"I think she had T-shirts printed with that slogan on." Anna forced a laugh. "I'm on a career break at the moment. I realised I was just going through the motions, and I want to find something with more meaning. A bit like you, I suppose."

"I'm really pleased for you, Anna. I always thought you were meant to do something more with your life."

"You don't know me, anymore, Jamie. I might be all about designer shoes and expense accounts, for all you know."

"Not my Anna."

"At least someone thinks I'm not a complete idiot for jacking in a job like that." She couldn't acknowledge his term of endearment. He was just slipping back into the language he'd always used, that was all. "But what did you mean when you said you wanted to put right the wrongs you'd done. You weren't just talking about us, were you?"

"No, like I said, I'm truly sorry for that. But I did some things because I was Lord Harrington's son, because I could get away with it. I was untouchable, treating other people the way my sense of entitlement told me I could. It was wrong. I panicked one day that I was turning into a carbon copy of my dad, who still looks down on the rest of the world like they're beneath him. I felt like I was suffocating, and I had to get away. I didn't want him to know where I was going, and so I couldn't risk telling you, even though it was the hardest thing I've ever had to do. I wanted you to come with me, I really did, but then you'd have to tell your mum and dad where you were, and my dad would have found a way of worming it out of them."

"My mum's never needed a lot of working on to spill a secret." She squeezed his hand, a ghost of her own laid to rest.

He hadn't left to get away from her, or because he thought she wasn't good enough for him, something that had eaten away at her for years afterwards. And he wasn't saying it just to be nice, she could see he meant it just by looking at his face. She'd seen that look before, the first time he'd told her he loved her, when they'd been walking barefoot across the sand late one summer's evening, when everyone else had packed up their buckets and spades and left them to a world of their own. Seventeen year olds weren't supposed to know what love was, but she'd been certain back then that she did, and she hadn't felt anything close to it since.

"Jamie! I need to talk to you." A booming voice carried across from the other side of the road, and Anna looked up to see Giles Harrington, Jamie's older brother, striding across the road towards them. He hadn't changed a bit. He'd always seemed to be permanently clad in a wax jacket, with floppy Hugh Grant style hair that he tossed around in the way a Disney princess would be proud of. "Little Anna Byron! Is that really you?"

"Giles, it's good to see you." She stuck out her hand, but he ignored it, making a big show of kissing her on both cheeks instead.

"Still the prettiest girl in St Nicholas Bay, even wearing a coat that makes you look like you robbed a charity shop in the dark." He winked at her, and she wanted to laugh. Giles had always fancied himself as a bit of a playboy, and it had worked on more than his fair share of women, according to Jamie, but Anna had never seen the appeal herself. "And I hear you're doing frightfully well, too, working for Grayson, Hamilton and Jones. Who'd have thought little Anna would fly so high?"

"Actually I was just telling your brother that I've handed my notice in."

"Oh, really?" He raised an eyebrow. "Who will you be working for?"

"I'm not sure, yet. I just fancied a change."

"Some chap break your heart, did he?" Giles gave a hearty laugh. Would it really be that amusing, if it were true?

"I don't know why everyone 'round here seems to think I can't make a decision without it having something to do with a man." She could only stand so much patronising.

"Actually, Anna wants to do something more meaningful with her life." Jamie gave his brother a pointed look, and Giles threw his hands up into the air.

"Oh, just what the world needs, another bleeding heart!"

"What did you want me for?" Jamie narrowed his eyes, his tone of voice changing completely and a muscle twitching in his cheek. His relationship with Giles didn't seem to have mellowed with time. They'd never had much in common, from what Anna could remember, and she could only imagine how Giles must have reacted to his younger brother's decision to train as a vicar. That must have made her parents' disappointment seem like nothing, at all.

"The bloody events director's walked out. God knows why!" Giles threw up his hands again. There were clearly a lot of people who exasperated him.

"I think you know why. Convincing women into bed with you by promising them the earth, and then not delivering on any of those promises, is hardly a way to persuade staff to be loyal to you." Jamie sound world-weary, as if it was a conversation they'd already had a thousand times.

"Don't come over all pious with me, little brother, just because you're wearing that ridiculous get up now." Giles gestured towards Jamie's dog collar. "We both know you've had your share of fillies in the past."

"Fillies?" Jamie shook his head, and his hand brushed against Anna's, sending a jolt of recognition through her body. Her reaction was just muscle memory, though. Wasn't that what it was called, when the body reacted to something all by itself, just because it had happened so many times before? "Apart from telling you to stop using such offensive terms to describe people, I don't know what you expect me to do about it?"

"I thought you might know someone who's looking for a job. After all, you must be right at the heart of the St Nicholas Bay grapevine now. I just need someone with a bit of a PR background, to oversee the major December events, like the Christmas fayre, the meet-and-greet days with Santa, and the mid-winter ball. It wouldn't be full time." Giles's eyes suddenly widened, and it was almost as if a lightbulb had switched on. "What about you, Anna? Didn't you just say you were between jobs?"

"I did, but ..." She hesitated, looking from Giles to Jamie and back again.

"She doesn't want to work for you, Giles. No-one does." Jamie spoke to him in the sort of straight-to-the-point way that only siblings could get away with.

"I think she's old enough to make her own decisions, aren't you, Anna?" Giles wasn't giving up easily. "You blew your chance to have any influence on her when you ran off to join the God squad."

"So nice to know I have your respect." Jamie narrowed his eyes again, and she wouldn't have put it past one of them to throw a punch. Thank God she had such a good relationship with Sara, despite how differently their mother had treated them. Jamie and Giles were like two stags butting heads.

"I couldn't commit to anything long-term, but there's a possibility it could work for both of us as a short-term solution." Maybe working up at the estate in the run-up to Christmas wouldn't be a bad thing. It would keep her out of the way of her mother and the constant questions about her next career move. Louise would be significantly cheered up by the prospect of telling her friends that Anna was working at Harrington Hall, too. It might also mean she'd get to see more of Jamie than she would otherwise. It definitely meant she'd get to see more of Giles than she wanted to, but nothing was perfect. "Okay, I'll help out at some of the events, but on one condition."

"Your wish is my command." Giles did a low bow, and Anna looked at the brothers again. How could the same parents create such different people?

"I can't be paid, because I'm on gardening leave, but I want to donate what you would have paid me to the Flashlight charity. They help homeless people all year round, but they've got a big project on at this time of year, making sure people have somewhere to stay and something to eat over Christmas."

"Not a very glamorous cause, is it?"

"All the more reason to support it." Anna crossed her arms, the ends of Jamie's sleeves flapping down towards her waist.

"Whatever you want. It'll be a pleasure to work so closely alongside you." Giles was obviously under the impression that he was being charming, but Anna's skin prickled in response. She crossed her fingers under the cover of Jamie's sleeves that she hadn't just agreed to something she was going to regret. "Give me your phone, and I'll put my number in, so you can text and arrange an initial meeting up at the house."

Giles took her phone, and when he handed it back, she couldn't help smiling. He'd tapped in his contact details as *'The*

Good Looking Harrington Brother'. At least he had a sense of humour, so maybe it wouldn't be all bad. With another of his none-too-subtle winks, he sprinted back towards his Range Rover, and Jamie let out a long sigh.

"Don't let him railroad you into helping him out. Just text him and tell him you can't do it." It sounded more like a request than a suggestion, but she shook her head.

"If you'd met my old boss, Nigel, you'd realise that Giles isn't going to cause me any trouble I can't handle. Plus, it'll please mum to hear I'm working for the estate, not to mention raising some money for Flashlight. Surely, you've got to approve of that?"

"Of course." Jamie looked at her for a long moment. "It's just that Giles is such a ..."

"Don't worry about me. I can look after myself." She laughed and pushed up the sleeve of the coat, so she could link her arm through his. Maybe they really could be friends this time around.

"Will you come to the church on Sunday?"

"Why?"

"So you can give me back my coat, of course!" It was his turn to laugh, the tension that had accompanied Giles's arrival finally leaving his face.

"Charming!"

"Seriously, I'd like to see you again. And maybe seeing me up there, in the pulpit, will finally convince you that all of this Reverend Harrington stuff isn't just some elaborate con trick. Not only that ..." He moved closer, until she could feel the warmth of his breath on her neck as he whispered in her ear, "I desperately need to boost the congregation!"

"I think you should be begging on your knees, after the way you left things the last time we were together." She shook her head. They'd both grown into different people since then, and she wanted this to be the last time she brought up the past.

She needed to boost her circle of friends, just as much as he needed to fill the pews. "But seeing as you can still make me smile, Jamie Harrington, I'm prepared to give one of your sermons a shot."

"I'll see you Sunday, then, Anna." His lips brushed against her cheek, before he turned back towards the church, and there was that same jolt of recognition.

Friendship might've been all she wanted, but her body was going to take some reminding of that.

Chapter Five

"So, remind me why we're going to church again?" Sara said, and Anna racked her brain to think of an answer that didn't have any connection to Jamie, even if his coat was draped over her arm.

"Because I need a bit of time away from Mum, and for once, she won't be at church, given it's the first day the Canterbury garden centre has got its Christmas lights on display." She squeezed Sara's arm. "And because you're a lovely big sister."

"I am. In fact, I'm so lovely that I'll pretend to buy into that and believe that our very easy-on-the-eye Reverend Harrington has absolutely nothing to do with your sudden interest in attending church."

"Sometimes, you're just as annoying as you were when you wouldn't let me borrow your lipstick. Remember, just before I started secondary school, and you always seemed to be getting ready to go out with Joe?" Anna grinned. Changing the subject might've been another strategy to avoid mentioning Jamie, but it was good to remember a time when her biggest challenge was persuading Sara to let her use that coral pink lipstick. She'd felt so sure it would make her look cool in front of her new secondary school friends. If only life was still that simple.

"I just wanted my little sister to stay little. In some ways, you'll always be that little girl to me." Sara stopped and pulled Anna close to her for a moment. She was quite a bit taller than Anna, and that forever made her feel like the big sister, even though the age gap had seemed to close over the years.

"What do you think I should do?" Anna twisted one of the buttons on Jamie's coat. Walking out of her job had seemed like a good idea, but she'd gone from school, to university, and straight onto a career path that she'd thought was all mapped out for her. To suddenly have choices again—and decisions to make—felt really strange.

“About Jamie? I think you should give him another try. After all, he was only eighteen when he disappeared on you, and he seems to have changed since he left. He’s very different to the other Harringtons.”

“I wasn’t actually talking about Jamie!” Anna shook her head. “I was talking about my next career move. And what makes you think Jamie even wants another chance?”

“Because every time I’ve seen him, since he came back, he’s found some way of bringing up your name.”

“He was probably just making conversation.”

“I’ll have you know that I’m very good at small talk, so he didn’t need to use you as a conversation starter.” Sara laughed. “As for what you should do career-wise… I know you mentioned maybe doing some charity work, but if you could do anything, what would it be? Just answer, don’t overthink it. It’s how I made the decision to retrain as a midwife.”

“Make a difference.”

“Okay. That’s a start. Maybe you should think about retraining, too?”

“I don’t think I’m cut out for hands-on care.” Anna wrinkled her nose. “I’m far too squeamish!”

“Oh, I know. I’ve seen you cleaning up after George. I’ve never seen anyone empty a litter tray wearing a balaclava before!”

“I’m not that bad!”

“Hmmm.” Sara raised an eyebrow. “I wasn’t thinking about nursing, or anything like that, anyway. I don’t know, maybe social work, or counselling, or something?”

“Do you think Mum would approve?”

“Does it matter? I don’t know why she’s got such a bee in her bonnet about your job, anyway. All I’ve ever wanted for Liam and Jade is to do something that makes them happy. But that’s never been enough for Mum. Not with me, anyway.”

"I get the feeling she regrets not doing more with her own life, and I guess she felt she had a second chance through us."

"Yeah, and then I let her down by getting pregnant. So it was all up to you." Sara stopped as they reached the porch of the church. "But I just want you to be happy, too, Anna, and I know you haven't been for a long time."

"Sara! You're the last person I expected to see here." Sara's best friend, Kate, came out of the church, gripping tightly to her little boy, Charlie's, hand. "And it's lovely to see you again, Anna, it's been ages. If you'll be home for the wedding and christening, we'd love to have you along."

"I'm planning to be here for a while. So, if you're sure you don't mind, I'd love that." She'd always liked Kate, and it was typical of her to include Anna in her wedding celebrations.

"We'd love to have you there." Kate turned towards Sara. "You haven't come just to hear the banns read, have you?"

"I'd like to say I have, but I think you'd see straight through me." Sara hugged her friend, and Charlie took the opportunity to try and break free, so his mother had to scoop him into her arms. "Anyway, where are you going? Doing a runner, before the banns are read and you're stuck with Will for life?"

"I think you know we're already stuck with each other, married, or not! I was just going to let your soon-to-be godson run off a bit of steam in the play-park, before the service starts. Patsy Bell has hemmed Jamie into one corner of the church to give him the benefit of her advice about what needs to change, now he's taken over."

"Poor Jamie." Sara sighed and turned to Anna, who realised again how out of touch she'd become with life in St Nicholas Bay. She'd never even heard of Patsy Bell. "You remember Patsy, don't you?"

"No, I think she must have moved into the Bay after I left."

"You'd probably remember her as Patricia Dean."

"Mean Dean?" Anna shuddered.

Patricia had lived next-door-but-one to their parents at one time, and Anna had never forgotten the time she'd hit a tennis ball so hard, it had sailed over next door's garden, and straight into Miss Dean's prizewinning roses, breaking a piece of trellis. Anyone would have thought Anna was a mass murderer, the way Patricia had carried on. She'd had to pay for some replacement trellis out of her pocket money, which had been fair enough. But Miss Dean had never let her forget it, and had referred to her as *'that out of control child'* every time she'd spoken to her mother. Anna had taken to going the long way round, when she got off the school bus back from the grammar school, just to avoid going past Patricia's house. Funnily enough, it was how she'd ended up meeting Jamie, when he'd saved her from the unwanted attentions of some local boys.

"That's her!" Sara twisted her mouth. "She's mellowed a bit, mainly after she got married, but she can still be a bit of a ..."

"Cow?" Kate smiled. "Sorry, I probably shouldn't say that, as I'm technically still in church, but at least it's not a lie."

"Someone actually married her?" Anna couldn't get her head around that either. There really was someone for everyone, just like her nan had told her at the grand old age of fourteen, when she'd been the last one at school to get a boyfriend.

"Yes, Barry was a lovely guy, and Patsy changed a lot, for a while. Sadly, he died last January, and her behaviour has gradually started to go downhill again." Sara exchanged a knowing look with Kate. "Put it this way, she objected that the children from Kate's class were making too much noise at the Harvest festival."

From what Anna remembered, Kate taught part time at the primary school in the Bay and worked with children who had special educational needs. It seemed Mean Dean hadn't changed that much, after all.

"I nearly lost my temper with her that day, but I keep reminding myself she's been through a lot over the years. Anyway, I better let this one run off some steam, or Patsy will go into orbit, if he kicks off in the service." Kate put Charlie back down, but kept her firm grip of his mitten-clad hand as they walked towards the play-park next door to the church, calling over her shoulder as she went, "I'll probably just slip into the back, if Jamie has started the service by the time I get back in, but hopefully we'll have a chance to catch up properly afterwards."

****

Jamie had just managed to extricate himself from Patsy Bell, when Anna walked into the church.

Patsy had seemed determined to interrogate him about his plans for the church over the Christmas period, and then proceeded to tell him he was doing it all wrong. He knew from looking through some of the notes his predecessor had left behind that Patsy's late husband, Barry, had been very involved in the Christmas celebrations in the past. With a name like Barry Bell, it seemed fitting that he'd organised the bell ringing and the choir, both of which had petered out after his death. When Jamie had mentioned to Patsy that he'd like to start up the choir again—the bell ringing might be a step too far for a while—she'd taken it as a personal insult. As if someone stepping into Barry's old role would somehow diminish the work he'd done. Although Jamie had tried his best to persuade her that it would be more like a legacy from Barry, she hadn't seemed convinced, and seeing Anna's face had lifted the weight off his shoulders.

Difficult parishioners were part of the job. He'd been warned often enough that there'd be those who felt they should make all the decisions in the church, and others who would want to take up more of his time than he could give. He had a feeling Patsy Bell might fulfil both roles.

But he hadn't been sure that Anna would even turn up. So, when she'd smiled and given a half wave, as she and Sara had taken their seats, her dark brown eyes as warm as he remembered, he'd felt ready to face a room full of Patsys.

With only two Sundays until advent, there were a lot of announcements to be made about upcoming events at the church over the Christmas period, so he planned to keep the sermon short. He'd just stepped up to the pulpit, when the church door creaked open, and a man who looked to be in his early fifties slid into a pew at the back of the church.

Some of the congregation turned around, to see who'd overslept and crept in late, and there was what felt like a collective intake of breath, followed by some furious whispering. Whoever the latecomer was, it was clearly a surprise that he was in church. Patsy's mouth was set in such a tight line, her lips had all but disappeared.

Jamie looked at Anna, who shrugged her shoulders, her expression changing as Sara whispered something in her ear. He could hardly stop the sermon to find out what was going on, so he pressed on, but he had the feeling the latecomer was the only one actually listening to him. Everyone else was intermittently turning around and sneaking glances at the man sitting in the last pew on the left, who was completely nondescript, other than his very bushy beard. About half way through the sermon, Katie returned with Charlie and slid in next to the man, laying a hand on his shoulder and having a quick whispered exchange.

Two hymns and a collective prayer later, Jamie was relieved to get to the notices, the first of which was to read out the banns for Kate and Will. There were only three Sundays left until their wedding and the joint christening service for Charlie. It could have been a special moment to share with the congregation, if only they'd listen. For all he knew, the guy who'd turned up late could be famous. He was so out of touch with popular culture, Jamie probably wouldn't know a celebrity if he met one.

He cleared his throat. At least Kate and Will might pay attention to the next bit. "I publish the banns between William James Osbourne and Katherine Charlotte Harris." As he watched Will twist in his seat to look at his fiancée and son at the back of the church, they seemed like a match made to last. During his training he'd wondered how he'd deal with a couple he didn't think were suited. He'd carried out pre-wedding counselling for several couples, during the time he'd been able to conduct weddings, but he knew Kate and Will had made sacrifices to be together, and their love for little Charlie was a tangible bond. He was going to enjoy officiating at their wedding. "This is the first time of asking. If any of you know any reason in law why they may not marry each other, you are to declare it." There was a pause, and the predictable nervous laughter which always seemed to accompany that question. "I'm sure we'd all like to take a moment at this point to offer our individual prayers for Will and Kate's marriage, as they take this first step in preparing for the rest of their life together." He paused for another minute, before adding, "Amen."

"Congratulations, Kate and Will!" Sara stood up and started a round of applause, one that not all of the congregation seemed keen to join in with. It wasn't exactly traditional, but it was a nice touch.

If it were possible, though, Patsy Bell's mouth set itself into an even thinner line.

Sadly, Jamie's next announcement was unlikely to improve her mood.

"Thank you, Sara, for expressing what I'm sure everyone was thinking." He glanced at Anna, and she rolled her eyes, gesturing towards Sara with a subtle tilt of her head. "This brings me to the next thing I wanted to talk about, before I go on to the rest of the notices. I'm sure no-one can fail to notice that Christmas is on the way. And with the Christmas tree lighting only two weeks away, and Will and Kate's wedding a week after that, I thought it would be the ideal time to see if we could start the St Nicholas Church choir up again. It's been almost a year since there's been one here, or for the services at the Chapel."

"You don't seriously think you could get a choir up and running in the next fortnight, do you? It's far more complicated than that." Patsy actually stood up to speak, her arms resolutely crossed.

"I'm not expecting us to win any prizes, but even if we could master one, or two, carols, and perhaps *Amazing Grace* for the wedding, I thought it would be a good start to getting the choir back to where it once was under the excellent leadership of your husband, Mrs Bell."

"I'd love to do it for Kate and Will's wedding. You'd do it, too, wouldn't you Anna?" Sara nudged her sister so hard, that Jamie actually saw her slide along the pew.

She widened her eyes and nodded, and that was the decision made. If Anna was prepared to be involved, then they were doing it, however much Patsy might protest.

Sara didn't seem to be finished, though. "I'm sure Nancy Williams will do as much as she can, with the baby due so soon. She usually runs the amateur dramatic group, but she's on maternity leave at the moment, so she's got the right sort of experience."

"Well, if we're going to avoid it being a *total* disaster, then I suppose I'll have to join, too." Patsy made it sound like she was saving human kind itself, and Jamie allowed himself a small smile. She'd given in much more quickly than he'd expected.

"That's great. I'm sure your experience will be invaluable to the choir, Mrs Bell." He offered up a prayer that she wouldn't make it unbearable for the rest of them. "Is there anyone else who feels they'd like to join us? I think we'll need to practice three, or four, times a week, to start with, to make sure we're ready to sing at the tree lighting and the wedding. Then, perhaps, we can reduce that to a couple of times a week." He was pushing it saying four times a week, with people as busy as they were at this time of year, but he wanted the choir to be able to carry off the songs. The fact that he'd get to see a lot of Anna had nothing to do with it.

"We'd like to join." The older of two teenage girls, sitting with their parents near the front of the church, put up her hand. "I'm Bethany, and this is Mollie."

"That's fantastic." Jamie breathed out. They probably had just about enough people to make it work, but they could use some male voices. "Anyone else? One of you gents must have a handsome baritone you want to show off?" As Jamie scanned the congregation, a lot of the men suddenly seemed very interested in staring down at their hymn books.

"I'd like to join, if I'm allowed to?" The man who'd caused such a stir when he'd arrived late spoke up. If his speaking voice, deep and strong, was anything to go by, he'd be perfect.

There was another gasp at his request, and Patsy shook her head violently.

"I think having a male voice in the choir would add something really special," Jamie said. "I don't think we've met before? I'm Jamie Harrington, I took over from Reverend Johns a couple of months ago."

"I'm John Casey. I remember you from when you were a teenager. Although, I'm sure you wouldn't remember me." The man held up his hand in greeting.

"Great to see you again, John, and even better to hear you'll be joining the choir. If anyone else thinks they might like to join, or has any other suggestions about the choir, then please let me know afterwards." Jamie hoped the wobble in his voice hadn't betrayed his shock at hearing that name again.

John Casey was a blast from the past he'd much rather have left there. He held up his hand, as Patsy opened her mouth to speak, and launched into the rest of the notices before she had the chance. He knew all too well who John Casey was. He could hardly forget that name—it had kept him awake at night for years. But the older man had been right, when he'd said that Jamie wouldn't recognise him. Whatever Patsy Bell personally had against John, he hoped it had nothing to do with the death of John's wife. Hadn't he been through enough already?

Jamie listed the rest of the upcoming events, and asked for some more volunteers to run stalls at the church's Christmas fair, as well as reminding everyone about the 'pack a shoebox' event, sending toys out to the orphanage he'd worked in when he was in India.

Patsy still looked ready to throttle him, even after all of that.

After reading the final prayer, he headed towards the doors at the side of the church, where some of the volunteers were setting up a trestle table to offer tea, coffee and biscuits, for a small donation towards church funds.

Patsy was down the aisle and standing next to him in a time that would have impressed an Olympic sprinter. "Reverend Harrington, you can't be serious about allowing John Casey to join the choir." She made no attempt to keep her voice down.

"I think we should talk about this somewhere else, don't you?"

"Why? Everyone knows he got away with murdering his wife. At least he had the good grace to disappear. But now he's turned up here, and not only has the barefaced cheek to come into church, of all places, but actually wants to join the choir."

"I really don't think this is the right place to talk about this." Jamie tried to lay a hand on Patsy's arm, but she shrugged it off, and he shot John an apologetic look.

"Don't worry, Reverend Harrington, it's probably best to get this all out in the open. I'm sure Mrs Bell isn't the only one thinking it. She's probably just the only one prepared to say it to my face." John took a couple of steps towards them. "As most of your congregation already know, my wife drowned ten years ago. I wasn't charged, because the police decided it was an accident, but more importantly, I wasn't charged because I wasn't even with Elizabeth that night, and I had absolutely nothing to do with her death. Unfortunately, not everyone seems willing to believe that." He looked pointedly at Patsy.

"So, why did you run away, then?" Patsy folded her arms across her chest again.

John was right. Whatever anyone thought about Patsy, she wasn't afraid of confrontation.

"I didn't *run* away. I just wanted to get away from the memories of this place, and the whispers and stares from people who chose to believe the worst about me."

"What about the state of your marriage? I suppose that was all lies, too?" Patsy's words were barbed.

Jamie decided it had gone too far already. "Mrs Bell, I think you should stop there. The police are the best people to determine someone's guilt, or innocence, and I'm sure they thoroughly investigated Mrs Casey's accident. If you don't feel able to work with Mr Casey in the choir, then that's your decision, but I don't want to hear any more rumours. We're a community, and we're here to support one another, not point fingers and gossip. It isn't the Christian thing to do." It would have been the Christian thing to tell everyone what had *really* happened that night, but it wouldn't bring Elizabeth Casey back, and it was a burden Jamie had decided to live with a long time ago.

Sara came and stood between Patsy and John. "Absolutely, Reverend."

Anna arrived next to her sister. "I think Mr Casey will make a great addition to the choir, and neither Sara, nor I, have got a problem with that, at all."

When she smiled up at Jamie, he felt something twist in his stomach. Was he going to lie to her again? He had no choice. If he told her why he'd really left so suddenly, she'd never forgive him.

"We're fine with it, too." Bethany tugged her sister's arm. "Aren't we Mollie?"

Mollie nodded shyly, and Patsy sighed so deeply, it was as if she'd sucked half the air out of the room.

"Well, with these youngsters in the choir, I'd better be on hand to make sure nothing untoward happens." Patsy shot John another look.

"Mr Casey, are you still happy to join the choir?" Jamie really hoped he would be. John deserved to be welcomed back into the community, and it would be entirely down to Jamie's silence, if he wasn't.

"John, please. I'd much prefer it if everyone called me John." He held out his hand to shake Jamie's. "And I'd like nothing better than to join the choir. I've been in an acapella group for the last five years, so I might even have some skills to bring to the table."

"Hmm, I hear they have some good choirs in prison." Patsy just couldn't seem to help herself.

"Mrs Bell, if you can't be civil towards John, I'm afraid you won't be able to join the choir."

"It's fine." John held up his hand. "Like I said, at least Patsy has the courage to say what she thinks. But, actually, the acapella group I was in raised money for a charity for homeless people. Maybe that's something we could do, if we get good enough to warrant donations?"

"I'd love that!" Anna's eyes lit up.

Jamie had always loved the way her whole face seemed to show when she was really happy about something. It was just one more thing he'd missed. "I think that's a great idea. So, how about we meet for our first session on Tuesday evening, say eight pm in the church?" Jamie avoided looking at Patsy again. "I'll even push the boat out and put the heating on for a bit, before you all arrive."

"You know how to spoil us, Jamie." Sara laughed.

"See you then, and before I forget, here's your coat." Anna turned towards him, their hands touching briefly as she handed him his jacket.

He'd have given almost anything to hold her hand again, like he had hundreds of times in the past. He'd taken it all for granted back then, and he didn't deserve someone like Anna, anymore. Not after what he'd done.

"Thanks. See you on Tuesday." Ignoring the tension still brewing between Patsy and John, Jamie watched her leave through the double doors at the side of the church—the sea just visible in the distance across the church yard. It was hard not to run after Anna. The urge to tell her everything was almost overwhelming. Maybe it had been a mistake to set up the choir. What if he couldn't hide the truth from her, when they were seeing each other so often?

He hadn't expected her to move back home when he'd taken the job, or dreamt that she'd want to join the choir. But maybe God had a plan. If he couldn't trust himself anymore, he'd just have to trust in a higher power.

Chapter Six

Anna came downstairs at half-past seven on Tuesday morning, to find her mum already surrounded by rolls of wrapping paper, ribbon, a huge dispenser of cello-tape, and a stack of shopping bags piled on the kitchen table. "Mum, what are you doing?"

"Dancing the tango. What does it look like I'm doing?" Louise didn't even look up. She'd definitely been shorter with Anna since she'd found out about her leaving her job.

George wandered over and jumped up on the chair next to Louise, meowing loudly, but somehow she managed to ignore him, too.

"I know what you're doing, I mean *why* are you doing it? Who wraps presents first thing on a Monday morning when we're still in November?"

"You're as bad as your father, thinking Christmas happens all by itself." Her mother finally looked up. "Why are you all dressed up like someone who's got a job to get to?"

"Because I have." Anna turned her back to put the kettle on, but she heard the kitchen chair scrape back, and when she turned around, her mother was standing up.

"Why didn't you tell me?"

"I wasn't a hundred percent sure until last night that I was going to take it. It's only temporary, and not everyone I spoke to thought it was a good idea."

"Please don't tell me you've got a Christmas job working in one of the shops in the Bay!"

"Why? Would that be such a bad thing? I'd love to run one of those shops in the arches by the harbour." Anna loved the little artisan businesses that had opened in the arches, which had once been used by fisherman, under the promenade that led up from the beach towards the centre of St Nicholas Bay. If Anna had been able to make anything, or even had the skills to run a tearoom, she'd happily have invested all her savings into something like that. So, why her mother found the prospect of her taking a holiday job in a shop so demeaning, she'd never know.

"Because you're a high achiever. At least, you *were*."

"Thanks!"

"What is this job, then?" Louise returned to the task of wrapping the presents, clearly already losing interest in the answer.

"I'm working at Harrington Hall."

"Waitressing, or in the gift shop? Either way, it's a waste of your talent, Anna."

"Neither." A big part of her wanted to let her mother think that *was* what she'd be doing, but if knowing the truth lifted the atmosphere in the house in the run-up to Christmas, it'd be worth it. At least, that was what she told herself. "I'm going to be the Events Director for the key Christmas events up at the Hall." She hated herself for using the title that Giles had given the job, which she knew her mother would pick up on.

"Oh, darling. So, you're a director again?" Her mother was out of her seat in a split second, and she threw her arms around Anna.

"It's only until Christmas, and I'm actually volunteering, because I'm not allowed to take a paid job yet. Giles is going to donate my earnings to the Flashlight charity instead."

"Well, no-one needs to know that, do they?" Louise couldn't keep the smile off her face. "I always thought you'd end up as the Lady of Harrington Hall one day. Things might not have worked out with Jamie, but Giles is still single, isn't he?"

"Mum!" Anna had to laugh. Sometimes her mother almost left her speechless. "If Giles was the last person on earth, I still wouldn't have any desire to become the future Lady Harrington."

"What about trying again with Jamie, then? You two were always thick as thieves, and if Giles never marries ..."

"We're just friends, and that's all we'll ever be."

"We'll see." It was amazing how animated her mum had become in the last few minutes. "I heard there was a bit of a to-do at the church, with John Casey, of all people, turning up?"

"I'd forgotten all about what happened to his wife. It must have been just before Jamie left, and I went to university, so I think I was a bit self-absorbed." It had felt like she'd never get over Jamie leaving, at the time. She'd cancelled the deferral of her place at university for the gap year she and Jamie had planned, but never had. She'd needed to get away, and a new life at university had been her sole focus. She'd partied hard, and worked even harder, coming out with a first-class degree and a patched-up heart. "I think I missed most of the fall-out from the investigation afterwards. But, judging by Patsy Bell's reaction, anyone would have thought John had been caught in the act of shoving Elizabeth into the sea."

"There are lots of people in small towns like this who like to judge others." Her mother sighed, and Anna had a feeling she wasn't just talking about John. She seemed convinced everyone looked down on her job, and it was more and more obvious that she didn't want that for her daughters. It still didn't excuse the way she'd treated Sara, though.

"He seems like a lovely man," Anna said. "Do you think there's any chance he did it?"

"No, but there were rumours about Elizabeth having an affair. She was seen out with a much younger man, and a lot of people came to the conclusion that John killed her in a jealous rage."

"Maybe it was her lover? Or just an accident, like the police said?" It was such a tragic story, either way, and it felt wrong talking about John behind his back.

"I think the police know what they're doing, but you must remember what Patsy Bell's like. That woman has always thought she knows better than anyone else. She actually had the nerve to ask me to add her house to my cleaning round." Her mother shook her head. "As if I'd do that and have her telling people that not only was I *just* a cleaner, but a second-rate one at that!"

"There's nothing wrong with being a cleaner, Mum. Far better than being a miserable old busybody, like Patsy Bell."

"I feel sorry for her, in a way. She never had children, much less one who's a director at Harrington Hall. I can't wait to bump into her and pass on that little nugget!"

"And you can tell her how well Sara is doing at university at the same time."

"Unfortunately, she'll always have Sara pegged as a teen mum."

"What about you, Mum?"

"She's doing very well *now*. But let's not have that conversation again." Louise picked up a roll of wrapping paper, which gave her an excuse to avoid looking at Anna. Maybe it was best to leave it, for the time being. Her mother seemed to be making progress, of a sort, when it came to Sara, and rowing about it again probably wouldn't help. Hopefully, she'd see it for herself, eventually.

"Okay. I need to be at Harrington Hall by eight, for a breakfast meeting with Giles, so can I borrow the car, if you don't need it this morning, please?" She stroked George's head, and he nudged her hand again as soon as she stopped, but she didn't have time to make much of a fuss of him. He'd probably get his own back later, by digging his claws into her legs. He'd done that a lot, whenever she'd got back late from work in London, as if he was punishing her for keeping him waiting.

"Of course you can take the car, darling. My little business woman, off to a breakfast meeting!"

“It’s really not that impressive. When she’s on placement, sometimes Sara’s already helped bring several new lives into the world by this time of day.”

“Don’t forget to take lots of pictures of Harrington Hall, and tag me into them on Facebook. I want everyone to see what a beautiful place you’re working in.”

“See you later, Mum.”

Anna felt exhausted already, and she still had to face breakfast with Giles. He’d better not have any expectations that she’d be willing to audition for the role of Lady Harrington. She shuddered at the thought, although her mood lifted at the prospect of seeing Jamie later.

But then she remembered that Patsy Bell would be there, too.

Was it too early to go back to bed?

****

Harrington Hall was as spectacular as she remembered. There were eight huge Christmas trees lining the sweeping gravel driveway, where it curved close to the house. They were draped with lights, but you couldn’t see the full effect during the day. Someone had obviously been working hard to get the Hall ready for Christmas, and Anna felt sorry for her predecessor. Although, how anyone could succumb to Giles’s advances was a mystery to her. It must have been horrible to leave a job so close to Christmas, though, especially when the Events Director had probably been planning the festivities for months.

Anna had always loved coming up to the big house with her mum, in the run-up to Christmas. Giles had told her, when they’d arranged the breakfast meeting, that the meet-and-greets with Santa had become one of the Hall’s biggest earners. As a child, they’d just seemed magical to Anna. She’d met her fair share of department store and garden centre Santas over the years. Some of them had the elastic on their cotton wool beards visibly poking out underneath their hats, and cheap red suits that looked nothing like the *'real'* thing. The Father Christmas at Harrington Hall had been on another level altogether. If his beard and big belly weren't for real, then they certainly looked it. He knew things about Anna he couldn't possibly have known, if he wasn't the real Santa, too—like who her best friend at St Nicholas Bay Primary School was, and where she'd been on holiday the previous summer. She'd found out years later that her mum had been asked to give those details when she'd booked the slot over the phone, but at the time she'd been completely convinced that the Harrington Hall Santa was the real deal.

Anna parked her mum's car in a space at the side of the staff car park. It had taken the whole of the five-minute drive to start warming up, and she didn't want to get out—like taking a warm shower on a cold morning and not wanting to face getting dressed. Sparkles of frost still clung to the surrounding grass, but deep down, she knew it wasn't the cold making her reluctant to get out of the car. The last time she'd been up to Harrington Hall had been when Jamie had disappeared.

She'd been so desperate to find out if he'd really gone—so unwilling to believe, after all they'd said to each other, that he'd do it to her—that she just had to go up to the Hall to check. After she'd cried on one of the young housekeeper's shoulders for a good half an hour, Lord Harrington had eventually been called, and he'd been very blunt with her. Anna's cheeks burned at the memory. She just hoped Hugo Harrington's recent retirement from the post of Chief Executive of the Estate meant he spent most of his time in the private quarters of the house. Even though he almost certainly wouldn't remember the naïve little girl he'd labelled her as, she'd rather not see him if she could help it.

Anna knew there was a staff entrance at the side of the house; at least that's where it had been ten years before when

Jamie had snuck her into the Hall on a regular basis. It might have seemed an odd thing for a couple in their late teens to do, but they'd almost always ended up hiding out in the library, looking up all the places they'd wanted to visit together. It was romantic, though, with candlelit dinners, courtesy of Jean-Claude, the French chef, who had seemed to approve of their burgeoning romance almost as much as he'd delighted in deceiving Hugo Harrington.

The door was still there, painted in the same shade of grey, and her heart pounded against her chest, just as it had before. Back then, it had been a combination of terror that Lord Harrington would catch them sneaking in, and the sensation that had always accompanied having her hand in Jamie's. He'd wanted to keep their relationship from his father, because he'd said Hugo would find a way to spoil it. After Jamie had left, she'd wondered, for a long time, if the secrecy had been for some other reason.

Now, though, the butterflies were entirely down to first day nerves.

She pressed the buzzer, and it took less than ten seconds to get a response.

"Can I help you?" It was a woman's voice.

"Hi, I'm Anna Byron. I'm here to start as the Events Director. Hopefully, Giles ... Mr Harrington has let you know I'm arriving."

"Of course. I'll let you in."

She pushed against the door, which released with the buzzer, and stepped inside the large hallway, onto the flagstone floor. The smell of cinnamon filled the air, and a moment later, a woman with the friendliest smile Anna had ever seen rounded the corner and stuck out her hand.

"Miss Byron, it's lovely to meet you. I'm Emily Dubois, the head housekeeper."

"Anna, please. It's lovely to meet you, Emily. Is it okay to call you Emily?"

"Absolutely." She smiled again, and some of Anna's nerves melted away. "Mr Harrington has asked me to take you up to the library for your meeting. Would you like some tea, or coffee?"

"Tea would be great, thank you." She would have liked something stronger, if it hadn't been so early in the morning. The prospect of going back to the library had her heart pounding quicker than ever. Maybe she should've asked Emily for a paper bag to breathe into. It was ridiculous. She'd grown up since then, and it had been ten years since she'd even been inside the house, but the feelings were still powerful. That was the teenage years for you, when everything seemed so intense, but it was just that muscle memory again.

Emily led the way across the main entrance hall, where a huge Christmas tree filled the space. It was decorated in red, gold and green, and matched the garlands wrapped all around the bannisters.

Did Giles really need her help? Christmas at the Hall looked pretty much sorted, and the smell of cinnamon seemed to pervade the whole house, making her stomach rumble.

She didn't really need Emily's help to find the way to the library, she could do it with her eyes shut if she needed to. She'd dreamt about it often enough, in the first few months at university, and then every so often since then, out-of-the-blue. It always took her by surprise and left a strange sense of melancholy behind for the next few days. It would be good to get some closure, and for the first time that morning, she was glad she'd taken the job.

"Good morning, Anna!" Giles stood up and laid the broadsheet newspaper he'd been reading on the chair beside him. A huge spread of Danish pastries, croissants, fresh fruit, rolls, cheese and cold meats were set out on the table in front of him. "Is there anything else Emily, or her team, can get you for breakfast, before we start? Bacon and eggs, perhaps?"

"No, thank you. This is great." As she spoke, Giles gestured towards the empty seat opposite him, and Anna sat down. "The Hall looks ready for Christmas already."

"Superficially, yes." Giles took his seat. "Unfortunately, Christina, who was doing the job before you, seems determined to seek revenge."

"What do you mean?"

"Well, so far today, I've discovered that she's cancelled all three of the Santa Claus's we had booked for the meet-and-greets"

"There are three of them?" Her eyebrows shot up in surprise, and Giles laughed.

"Well, yes. There are employment laws about lunchbreaks and days off, you know, and, of course, we have to cover for sickness." Giles shook his head. "Luckily, I've been able to get hold of two of them, and they hadn't managed to get re-booked, but the other one had already agreed to a new job. We'll either have to find another Santa Claus—and believe me, they need to be the best—or we'll have to cancel some of the meet-and-greet slots."

"Oh, no, you can't do that!" Anna knew what that would have felt like to her as a child. "We can work something out. I'll put some calls out."

"It can't be just anyone, you know. We've been rated the highest Christmas attraction in the area for the last ten years, and I don't want that slipping."

"I know, and the Santa meet-and-greets have always been fabulous. They were the highlight of my Christmas as a child."

"Jamie and I never had that pleasure. It was always business for Dad, so we knew there was no such thing as the real Santa Claus for almost as long as I can remember. It became even more about the business once our mother passed away, and Jamie was only a baby, then." Maybe there was a hint of vulnerability about Giles, after all.

"I'll make sure the Santa Claus is perfect." It couldn't be that difficult, surely. "Are there any other issues?"

"We normally have a choir to close the Christmas fayre, but Christina cancelled them, too, and she was so rude about it that I haven't been able to persuade them to come back. Even when I told them why she'd done what she did."

"That must have been awkward!" She laughed, realising she was more able to relax around Giles than she'd expected.

"It wasn't the most pleasant conversation I've ever had."

"There might be something we can do. It would be great to have a local choir perform, wouldn't it?"

"Yes. We used to book Barry Bell's choir, but there's been nothing like it since he died."

"Well, there might be ..." Anna wondered if she should even mention it. Would they stand a chance of being good enough to perform in public in time? There was no guarantee anyone would even turn up to the first rehearsal.

Maybe it was tempting fate, but she couldn't stop herself. "Jamie's started a new choir. Perhaps we could perform, if the expectations aren't too high?"

"We? You're joining the choir." He gave her a slow smile. "The old fire's still burning for Jamie, then?"

"Of course not, it's ancient history." Anna tore the end off a croissant as she spoke, so she wouldn't have to make eye contact with Giles. "I've just been away for a long time, and I thought it would be good to do something in the community while I'm here."

"No chance of me persuading you to stay on, then?"

"I'm afraid not, but I will do the best job I can for you until Christmas. So, what do you think about the choir? What are you after?"

"Nothing spectacular. Just a couple of carols at the end of the fayre."

"I think we can manage that. What else do you want me to be getting on with?"

"Well, you've got an admin team, so you need to check that all the meet-and-greet bookings are going to plan with the right number of gifts ordered. You're overseeing everything, really. You need to look at the suppliers and vendors for the Christmas fayre, and make sure it's all in order, as well as with the ball. I just can't be sure any of the work Christina was doing hasn't been undone. I've never spent so much time on the phone, but I couldn't trust anyone else to do it. I'm still not convinced all of the staff are on side. Some of them were very close to Christina, so you'll need to keep a close eye on what your team are up to, as well."

"Sounds like this *part-time* job is going to keep me on my toes!"

"Nothing you can't handle, after working for Nigel Grayson."

"Ah, there you are Giles!" Hugo Harrington strode into the library, slap-bang into the middle of their conversation. His hair had turned completely grey, but he'd been dark like Giles the last time she saw him. From the photos she'd seen, Jamie's colouring was more like his mother's. "No wonder you're tucked away in here with this young lady. Don't let him convince you he's interested in more than your business capabilities. The staff turnover here is getting embarrassing."

"Thank you, Father. But I'm sure Anna can look after herself. You must remember Anna—she went out with Jamie for a couple of years, before he went off to find himself." Giles raised a questioning eyebrow, but despite wrinkling his nose at the mention of Jamie's disappearance, Hugo looked nonplussed. Probably because he hadn't known she'd been dating Jamie until after he'd left. "She's been working for Jeremy Grayson's son, Nigel, as a marketing director at his law firm."

"Really?" Hugo actually looked vaguely interested for a moment. "I went to university with Jeremy. He was a frightful bore all the way through. Can't imagine his son is all that different?"

"He had his challenges to work for." Anna was determined to remain professional. She'd need to find another job eventually, and bad mouthing a former employer was never a good move.

"So, what are you doing, hanging out in this backwater, then? Life in the city get too exciting for you?" Hugo picked up Giles's discarded paper and dropped it on the floor, like someone who'd spent a whole lifetime having other people to pick up after him. Taking a seat, he ripped open one of the rolls and spread it thickly with butter.

"I'm having a break while I decide what I want to do, and I thought I'd come home for Christmas. I wasn't planning to work, but then Giles made me an offer I can't refuse."

"I've already warned you about that!" Hugo didn't bother to wait until his mouth was empty before speaking, and Anna pushed her own croissant away, suddenly put off her breakfast.

"Actually, Giles agreed to donate to a homelessness charity in lieu of wages, as I'm still on gardening leave."

"He did *what*?" Hugo opened his mouth again, and Anna had to look away. "The bloody homeless? Layabouts and drug addicts, most of them."

Her scalp bristled at his attitude. If it wasn't for the amount of money going to the charity in lieu of her wages, she would have walked out. Hugo Harrington was every bit as obnoxious as she remembered, but she'd actually started to feel sorry for Giles. It went someway to explaining why he behaved the way he did. "All sorts of people end up on the streets. Sometimes, one bad decision, or a tragedy, can spiral into homelessness."

"They just need to get a job. It isn't rocket science." Hugo snorted, and his response would have been almost laughable, if it hadn't been so awful. Especially coming from a man who'd been born with everything and never had to worry a day in his life about not being able to pay a bill. He'd probably never even had to cook for himself.

"Well, I think I better get on. There's a lot to sort out, to make sure everything's in place for the fayre and the start of the meet-and-greets." Anna stood up. "If you'll excuse me, gentlemen. I'll go down and find Emily, and ask her to introduce me to the rest of the team."

"I can come with you." Giles looked at her, his eyes almost pleading, but she couldn't risk Hugo saying he'd come, too.

"No, that's fine. I'm sure you've got more important stuff to be getting on with."

"Yes, Giles, I need to talk to you about last quarter's figures. Very disappointing. I hope my decision to retire wasn't a mistake." Hugo gave his son a dismissive look, and Anna felt another stab of sympathy for Giles.

Heading back down the stairs as fast as she could, she finally allowed herself to slow down. She'd never been in this part of the house before, not legitimately, and it was truly beautiful. The Christmas tree reached almost up to the ceiling, just to the left of a huge chandelier that probably cost enough to fund a small charity for a year. As she walked back across the grand entrance hall, towards where she'd met Emily earlier, she saw a glimpse of one of the other rooms through an open door.

The stone fireplace was draped with another beautiful garland, and the scent of cinnamon mingled with ginger. It was like someone had bottled the smell of Christmas and was piping it through the entire house.

Emily suddenly emerged from the shadows, making her jump. "How did you get on?"

"Fine, thank you. I was wondering if you'd mind introducing me to the rest of the events team?"

"Of course." Emily paused before she spoke again, as if she was weighing something up. "You don't remember me, do you? I've had two children since we met, and gained at least a stone with each one, and plenty of grey hairs."

Anna's cheeks burned, a horrible realisation striking as she looked at Emily again. "It was you, wasn't it? That time I came to the house, looking for Jamie?"

"One and the same. I wasn't sure whether to mention it, but I thought enough time had passed now."

"You were so lovely to me. I never forgot it, even if I didn't recognise you. Although, I had so much mascara streaming down my face that day, I don't think I'd have recognised my own mother."

"You were such a sweet, little thing, and I felt so sorry for you. My husband always hoped you might find a way to work it out. He said you were meant to be together."

"Your husband?"

"Yes, Jean-Claude. Do you remember him? Because he remembers you! He was really pleased when I told him Mr Harrington had persuaded you to work here over Christmas."

"Of course. Does he still work here? I didn't even know he was married."

"He wasn't back then, but I was determined he would be eventually!" Emily smiled again. "Now we've got two children, and he runs his own restaurant in the Bay. The only reason I'm still here is because I love the house so much. And I'm worried that if we work together and live together, it might end with a murder!"

"Please give Jean-Claude my love, and I'll definitely go and see him in the restaurant. The meals he used to cook for me and Jamie were amazing."

"He'd love that. Now, let me introduce you to everyone, and I'll tell you who you need to look out for. Mr Harrington is a bit worried about some of them."

"Yes, he said that. And thank you, so much."

Following Emily to where the offices were situated at the back of the house, Anna felt the tension drain out of her. She'd wanted to make new friends, and it felt like she was already half way there with Emily. Giles wasn't nearly as bad as she'd feared, either, and it was shaping up to be a much better day than she'd expected.

****

Jamie must have looked at his watch a hundred times, before the meetup for the choir finally came around. Bethany and Mollie were first to arrive, and they busied themselves with their mobile phones while they waited for everyone else to turn up.

Patsy arrived next and didn't hesitate in making her presence felt. "Phones in church, really?"

"Sorry." Mollie mumbled an apology and slid her phone into her coat pocket, but Bethany ignored her altogether.

Jamie liked her style.

John Casey arrived next, a blast of cold air following him in as he opened the church doors, and Jamie walked over to turn the heating up. "Good evening, everyone."

"Hi, John, good to see you." As Jamie spoke, the door opened again, and Anna, Sara and Nancy came in.

They'd obviously managed to persuade their friend to join the choir, as hoped, and as Nancy ran the amateur dramatics group, she was definitely a good addition. Someone else followed them in, too, who Jamie hadn't met before, but it looked like they might have another male voice.

"Reverend Harrington, this is Jack, my husband." Nancy introduced him to Jamie. "He's going to be Charlie's godfather, and he's come to join the choir, too."

"Did I have a choice, then?" Jack looked like he might head for the door, if he was given the chance.

"Not if you know what's good for you." Nancy nudged him and pulled down the jumper she was wearing, which had ridden up over her baby bump.

"Looks like I'm here to stay, then! Pleased to meet you, Reverend Harrington."

"Likewise, Jack, and please, call me Jamie." He turned towards Anna and smiled. He wanted to ask how her first day working up at the Hall had gone, but that would have to wait. "Okay, I think we've got everyone we're expecting now. I thought we could start by having everyone sing a verse of one of the carols we want to perform, to see if we can work out how to arrange the group, and who might be up for the solos."

"So, you're taking charge of the choir?" Patsy raised her voice above the chatter that had broken out about the prospect of solos. "I thought you wanted my help."

"I do. I want everyone's help, but someone needs to take overall responsibility." Jamie kept his tone level, despite the expression on Patsy's face. "And since I'm definitely not going to be the best singer in the room, it might as well be me."

"Good idea." Anna cut in, before Patsy could reply. "And since you're in charge, I wanted to ask if the choir might be able to add an additional performance to the schedule? Giles is looking for a choir to sing a couple of carols at the end of the Christmas fayre. The group he'd booked are ... unexpectedly unavailable."

"Well, if everyone's in agreement?" Jamie glanced around, and no-one seemed to have any objections. Even Patsy looked relatively enthusiastic about the idea. He only wished he felt a bit keener himself.

For the most part, the auditions went as expected. Nancy was a good singer, and an even better performer. Jack, Anna, and Sara could all carry a tune, but none of them wanted, or warranted, a solo. Patsy wasn't nearly as good a singer as she thought she was, but John had a rich baritone. He and Nancy were definitely the front runners for the solo spots, until Bethany and Mollie stepped forward. Bethany had a good voice, and like Nancy, she was a really confident performer, but it was Mollie who turned out to be the big surprise. She was the quieter of the two sisters but, when she opened her mouth to sing, everyone stopped what they were doing. Even Patsy took the sour-lemon-sucking expression off her face to watch Mollie.

"I think we've found our lead soloist," Jamie said, once the spontaneous round of applause had died out. Her mum had said she wanted to build up Mollie's confidence, but he'd never expected her to sound like that. "Nancy, Bethany, and John, if you're willing to perform some solos, too, I think that could work well? With everyone else on harmonies."

"Sounds good to me." Sara responded first, and the rest of the group nodded, except Patsy, whose mouth was set in a thin line again. If she walked out of the choir because of it, then it was something Jamie would just have to accept. He didn't want to deliberately upset anyone, but he couldn't spend the next month, or so, just trying to keep Patsy happy.

"Right, well, let's look at some carols and decide which of them we're going to focus on perfecting. I know I originally said we'd only go for two, or three, but I'm hoping, given the level of ability in the group, we might be able to extend that."

The next hour passed so fast, it was a surprise to realise how late it had got. "I think we'd better call it a night, for now," Jamie said. "Thanks, everyone."

He was amazed at how well they'd done—they might actually be able to pull the whole choir thing off, after all. Everyone seemed to be working really hard, although he couldn't help wondering if some of that was aimed at proving Patsy wrong. They were all being extra friendly to John, too, except for Patsy, who shook her head every time she looked in his direction, or someone else spoke to him. For his part, John seemed able to rise above it, but Jamie would have to keep an eye on the situation.

"If anyone wants to stay for a tea, or coffee, I'll put the kettle on." Jamie's eyes drifted towards Anna, despite his best intentions, and he smiled when she nodded.

"I'll text dad to come and pick us up, but it'll probably take him at least twenty minutes. We don't really drink tea, though, do we Moll?" Bethany looked at her sister, who shook her head.

"I think there's some squash in the church kitchen." Jamie fought the urge to laugh, wondering if he'd ever sounded so uncool—remembering, for a moment, what it'd felt like to be that age and nearly dissolving into hysterics, when one of his dad's many girlfriends had referred to the charts as the hit parade. Of course, she hadn't lasted long, they never did, and she'd been far too close to his father's own age. "Or I've got some cans of Pepsi at the vicarage? I can go and get them, if someone can put the kettle on here?"

"I'll do it." Sara gave Anna a push towards him as she spoke. "And Anna can give you a hand with the Pepsis."

"Of course." Anna said, despite looking as though it wasn't an offer she'd intended to make.

Neither of them spoke, at first, as they walked towards the vicarage next door to the church.

"How was your first day?" Jamie broke the silence. "I hope my brother was on his best behaviour."

"Giles was fine. Your dad turned up at our meeting, too."

"That can't have been a lot of fun." Jamie unlocked the door to the cottage, and Anna followed him inside.

"He's an interesting character." Anna stood in the doorway of the kitchen, as he took the cans of drink out of the fridge.

She was beautiful, and just for a moment he could imagine what it would be like to share a house with her. Would it have lasted, their teenage romance, if things had been different? Probably not, but he wished they could have tried.

"He's not a nice man. I sometimes wonder if he was even before Mum died. Giles seems to think he was a lot better back then, but I can't remember that."

"It must be hard, not remembering your mum, either."

"People go through a lot worse."

"I think you handled things really well with Patsy tonight." As she spoke, Jamie walked towards her.

"She's been through a lot in the last year, or so, with losing Barry. She might drive everyone mad from time to time, but I think we should be patient with her, if we can."

"It's a shame I missed her nice phase." Anna gave a hollow laugh. "She was pretty horrible before I left for university. And although I came back for the holidays, I never really saw much of anyone but the family. Sara and Mum said the same, though, about her being quite nice when she was married to Barry."

"I think she's lonely. Whether they admit it, or not, most people want someone to love."

"What about you?" Anna's eyes searched his face, but the question put them on dangerous ground.

He didn't deserve a second chance with her, but it didn't stop him wanting one.

"I'm the same as everyone else." He took a deep breath. "I've missed you."

"I missed you, too, for a long time."

"And now?" Jamie tried not to think about everyone waiting for them back at the church. He needed to hear what Anna had to say.

"I'd be lying if I said I didn't feel a spark when I saw you again, but I think it's just the memory of what we had."

"You know the best way to test a theory, don't you?" He moved closer to her, and she tilted her head to look up at him.

"No."

“Challenge it.” He pressed his lips against hers.

There was no way it was just a memory, at least not for him. He still loved Anna. If he was honest, there wasn’t a moment in the past ten years when he hadn’t done. There’d been other girls in the early days, before he’d started his training, but none of them had even come close to her.

“I think I might have to test the theory again.” Anna whispered the words, as she pulled away. “But not now. The last thing I want is Patsy Bell bursting in here, to find out why we’ve been so long. I might never be able to kiss anyone again, if she does that.”

“Me, neither.” He laughed, not sure if it was due to the prospect of Patsy’s righteous indignation, or relief that Anna hadn’t rejected him outright. “I suppose we have to go back, then?”

“We do, but maybe we can meet up for lunch this week?”

“I know just the place.” Jamie followed her out of the cottage and across the churchyard, trying to contain the stupid smile he was sure had spread across his face.

Sara had done as promised and was carrying cups and saucers out of the kitchen, helped by John, as Jamie and Anna came back into the church. Patsy had her back to them and had corned Jack and Nancy.

“Of course, Reverend Harrington better warn his brother, if we’re going to perform at the Hall, that John Casey is going to be there with us, so he can lock up the silver, or maybe hide the knife block.”

At the mention of his name, John just shook his head.

Jamie handed the cans of Pepsi to Anna and gently took hold of Patsy’s arm, making her jump in response. “I’ve never had to throw someone out of my church before, but I’m prepared to make it a first, if you carry on like this, Patsy. I’ve warned you before.” The muscles in his jaw tightened as he struggled to maintain his composure. It would be easy for him to shut Patsy up by telling her the truth, but there'd be no going back from that.

"I ... I was just ..." Patsy spluttered.

"I know what you were just doing. John's a good man, and he's been through more than enough already. You, of all people, should know what that feels like."

"It's not the same."

"Have you ever actually spoken to John—properly, I mean? Instead of just sniping at him and repeating malicious gossip from people who've got nothing better to do?" Jamie's good mood was fast evaporating, as Patsy shook her head. "Do you understand me when I say, I won't tolerate hearing this sort of thing again, and I don't suppose Nancy and Jack want to hear the poison you're spouting, either."

"I've got the message, Reverend." She still couldn't quite bring herself to apologise. "If you'll excuse me, I won't stay for tea." Snatching up her bag, Patsy disappeared through the double doors without a backward glance.

For the second time that evening, the rest of the choir burst into applause. Jamie only wished he deserved it. If they'd known the full story, they'd probably have lynched him, instead.

Chapter Seven

Anna and Jamie's planned lunch ended up being postponed twice. The first time, one of Jamie's parishioners was unexpectedly taken into hospital, and his wife was having problems getting in to visit him because she didn't drive. Seeing how willing Jamie was to put other people first just made Anna like him more. Despite her saying she needed to repeat the experiment, kissing Jamie had left her in no doubt that the physical attraction she felt for him was stronger than ever.

But he'd changed—a lot—too, and it seemed to be for the better.

The second lunch date was cancelled after a minor crisis at Harrington Hall. Monica, one of the admin team, who Emily had warned her to keep a close eye on, had managed to crash the computer system, and it looked as though they'd lost all the meet-and-greet Santa bookings. Apologising to Jamie, Anna had driven straight over to the Hall, where Giles looked ready to throttle Monica. For someone who'd made such a catastrophic mistake, Monica looked remarkably pleased with herself. It had taken Anna several hours, and a frantic phone call to one of the IT team at Grayson, Hamilton and Jones, who she'd been quite friendly with, to resolve the problem. She'd spent another couple of hours backing up all the systems to make sure it didn't happen again, and talking to Giles about how to handle Monica. He seemed convinced it'd been a deliberate attempt to sabotage business at the Hall, but since they had no actual proof—and technically anyone could make a mistake—they couldn't just fire her. Not without risking even more of a backlash. If Anna thought she'd left all the office politics behind her when she'd left the law firm, she'd been sadly mistaken.

Friday rolled around, and they'd already had another choir practice, before they finally managed to meet for lunch. Jamie drove Anna out to a quiet pub in the countryside, a few miles outside the Bay. It wasn't that they wanted to keep their relationship—if you could call it that—secret, but there seemed to be an unspoken agreement between them to keep things quiet, until they knew exactly what it was. Anna could only imagine her mother's reaction, if she thought there was a chance she might end up marrying into the Harrington clan, after all. Facing her mother's raging disappointment once in the past month had been more than enough.

"I thought we might never get this lunch." Jamie opened the door to the pub as he spoke, and the heat from the open fire roaring in the grate hit Anna as she stepped inside.

The ceilings of the pub were low, and Christmas decorations already hung from the beams. It was tasteful, though, with low-key white lights, garlands of holly, and even a couple of bunches of mistletoe. It might not have been December yet, but the Christmas get-togethers probably started as soon as the sparklers went out after bonfire night.

"I did wonder if you were avoiding me." Anna grinned.

"You were the one who cancelled last time, so you could be with my brother, instead."

"It sounds really bad when you put it like that!" She picked out a table in the corner of the dining area, away from the bar, where a group of men who looked like they hung out there every lunchtime were sitting. One of them had a laugh like the low rumble of thunder building up to a crescendo, and Anna didn't want to spend the hour, or so, she had with Jamie battling to talk over that.

"Would you think any less of me, if I told you I was envious of a database?" Jamie sat down opposite her.

"It wasn't exactly my idea of fun, either, but at least we managed to get it sorted."

"Giles was really impressed. He reckons you saved his neck. If he'd had to tell Dad what happened, and worse still, *why* it happened, he might have been disinherited."

"Does it mean that much to him? Putting up with the way your dad talks to him, just for the promise of getting his hands on the estate one day?" Anna clapped a hand over her mouth. "I'm sorry, I shouldn't have said that."

The arrival of the waitress, who handed them two menus, was a welcome distraction. "We've got a Christmas Special menu at the moment—that's the smaller one—as well as our main menu, and you can find the wine list at the back of that." Her ever-so-slightly bored tone suggested it was information she'd repeated far more often than she'd have preferred. "I'll come back and take your order in a few moments."

"I'm sorry..." Anna started to apologise again, as the waitress left.

"What? For being honest? That means more to me than anything." Jamie laid his hand on hers, and her body responded, as it did every time he touched her.

She'd only be fooling herself, if she kept insisting it was just a memory. If she'd been into playing games, she'd be making it far too easy for Jamie to come back into her life. But games didn't interest her, and she seemed to have even less control over her feelings than she'd had at eighteen anyway.

"You don't seem to have the same need to pander to your dad." She hadn't planned to say that, either, and she knew, as well as anyone, that no-one really understood the dynamics of a family unless they were in it.

"My dad and I reached an impasse years ago, and I was probably disinherited back then, too. At least, I hope so. He certainly cut off my allowance as soon as I left." Jamie had such an intense look in his eyes. If he didn't mean what he was saying, he missed his vocation as an actor. "It's different for Giles. As the eldest, he's always been in line to inherit the estate and the title, so it's hardly surprising that it's become his *raison d'être*. Like I said, I value honesty more than anything, these days."

"Well, you are a man of the cloth." She could still barely believe it.

"I'd like to say my thoughts are always pure, but since you came home ..."

"Reverend Harrington!" She feigned a look of indignation.

"I'm only human, and I'm going to have to look at this menu instead of you for the next few minutes, or I'm not going to stand any chance of fighting it."

After they'd ordered, Jamie seemed to make a concerted effort to change the subject, and talk soon turned to the choir.

"I was quite surprised Patsy even came back last night, but she seemed to be doing her best not to make too many digs about John. I don't know how he puts up with it."

The night before had given Anna her first proper opportunity to talk to John, when they'd volunteered to do the teas after the practice had finished. He had an air of sorrow about him, despite his attempts to make small talk. She'd wanted to tell him she believed he was innocent—that almost everyone did—but it might have made things more uncomfortable for him than not mentioning it at all. So, instead, they'd talked about the weather and their plans for Christmas. John was planning to help out at a soup kitchen in Canterbury, serving Christmas dinners to people who wouldn't get one otherwise. He'd told Anna and Jamie that his daughter couldn't make it back for Christmas, and he had no other family around. In some ways, there were quite a lot of similarities between him and Patsy.

Jamie nodded. "I think Patsy's trying, although she always looks like the next barbed comment is just below the surface. But I hope she manages to keep control of it, for her sake, as much as John's."

"Can you get over Mollie? Her voice gave me goose-bumps. I thought that was just a cliché, until I heard her sing."

"Bethany told me that her boyfriend heard Mollie singing in their garden last year, when she thought no-one was listening, and he's been trying to persuade her ever since to sing with his band." Jamie topped up Anna's wine glass. "Apparently, since Mollie got chosen to do the solo in the choir, she's actually been thinking more seriously about joining them. So it's been worth it, even for that."

"Do you think we'll be ready to perform? It suddenly seems like we've got no time at all until the tree lighting, and the Christmas fayre up at the Hall."

"I think we'll be fine, as long as everyone keeps making the effort to get to the practice sessions."

"Some of us only come to stare at the sexy new vicar, you know."

"Ah, so that's why Patsy was so willing to come back!"

They both laughed. He was still the same old Jamie, and she tried not to think about how close they were getting to the end of the year, too. She'd have to make a decision then about what she was going to do next, and where that might take her, but she didn't want to think about that yet.

"I thought we might be able to have some collection boxes at the tree lighting and Christmas fayre?" Jamie's voice brought her back to the present.

"For the church?"

"No, for Flashlight. You could add it to the funds that Giles is going to donate on your behalf. I know it means a lot to you."

"It does. In a weird sort of way, it brought me home." She put her fork down and looked across at him. "There was a young homeless guy outside my office building in London one day. When I spoke to him, I just had this realisation that I was wasting my life doing something I didn't believe in. I gave him some money I'd just have spent on a month of coffees otherwise, but it made such a difference to him."

"I know what you mean. I grew up in a family with more wealth than anyone needs to have, but I've felt so much richer since I started working in the community." Jamie screwed up his face. "Sorry, that probably sounds as cheesy as hell."

"I like cheese." Anna laughed again. It seemed so easy to do in Jamie's company. Something else she hadn't even realised she'd missed. "And I like the idea of raising extra money for Flashlight even more. I'm going to email them later, to see if Giles can pay the funds in lieu of my wages straight into their bank account. So I'll ask them if I can pick up some collection tins before the tree lighting. Although, Heaven knows what Patsy Bell's going to think of us collecting for a homelessness charity, but I can just imagine the look on her face!"

"I'm sure the sexy new vicar you mentioned can talk her round!" He dropped a perfect wink.

"Jamie Harrington, you're shameless!"

"And that's why you love me!" He was joking again, but if he'd asked her outright, she wasn't sure she'd have been able to deny it. He'd said he valued honesty above anything, and she really didn't want to let him down.

****

After Jamie had dropped Anna back at the end of her parents' road, he drove up towards the clifftop. It had been like going back in time—her insisting that he drop her at the end of the road, so there'd be less chance of them being caught sharing a goodbye kiss. He hadn't wanted her to go, at all, but he was desperately trying to go more slowly than his gut was telling him to.

Guilt was powerful antidote, though, and in a way, he was glad he had the meeting with the parish council lined up that evening. He didn't exactly relish parish council meetings, but at least it would give him and Anna a bit of breathing space. He wouldn't be able to make plans to see her over the weekend, either, what with the primary school's Christmas Fair on Saturday, and a wine and wisdom evening that night, plus a family service and a planning meeting for the church fair on Sunday. If he'd had a gap in his diary, he wouldn't have been able to resist asking Anna out again. He'd spend every spare minute with her if he could.

But he didn't deserve that, and he didn't deserve her, either. Not after he'd said he valued honesty above everything else. If she knew the truth, she'd probably have tipped her lunch in his lap.

He valued *her* honesty, though, even if that made him the world's biggest hypocrite.

Breaking things off with her before they got too involved might have been the right thing to do, but he couldn't bear to lose her again. Leaving her without saying goodbye had been the second biggest mistake of his life. He only hoped the even bigger mistake he'd made wouldn't stop him putting that right.

Chapter Eight

Sara came into the kitchen, a week or so after Anna's first proper date with Jamie, waving a blue photo album in the air. "Look what I found in the loft."

Their parents had gone for dinner with friends, along the coast in Whitstable, and Sara had come round to share a takeaway with Anna—although, her sister's first priority had been to find out how things were going with Jamie. Emily and Sara were the only ones who knew Anna and Jamie had rekindled their relationship, and one of the best things about being back home was rebuilding a close relationship with her sister.

She'd filled Sara in on the handful of dates they'd managed to fit in between Jamie's numerous commitments, her work up at the Hall and trying to avoid making their mum suspicious. While Anna was calling the Chinese restaurant to place their order, Sara had disappeared upstairs. As soon as she put the phone down, George started weaving in and out of her legs, as if he could sense that food was on its way.

"You've been up in the loft?" Anna could see the bits of loft insulation sticking to Sara's jumper. So, she didn't really need an answer to her question.

"Yes, I promised Mum I'd get the decorations down, to save Dad doing it. Although, I think he might have refused. You know what she's like. She's been chomping at the bit to put them up since October, but Dad always makes her hold out until the first weekend in December, if he can. They'll be up tomorrow, regardless."

"Why didn't she just ask me? I'm the one living here."

Sara shrugged in response, but they both knew the answer. Sara was the one her parents had always turned to for practical help, and Anna had assumed it was just because she lived close by. She just hoped they appreciated all the things Sara did for them.

"It's just because I've always done it, I suppose."

"Maybe she'll let me help decorate the tree." Anna caught Sara's eye, and they both laughed. "There's a first time for everything!"

Their mother had always taken charge of the decorating, and they'd both realised as teenagers that she'd pretended to let them help when they'd been younger, but had got up to re-decorate the tree after they'd gone to bed. Once they'd realised, they'd stopped wanting to help, and it had since become a standing joke.

Anna didn't rate Jamie's chances of deciding how the church should be decorated very highly, either.

"So, do you recognise this?" Sara set the photo album down on the kitchen table.

"Is it one of the albums I made up?" She'd studied photography for A-level, as a bit of light relief alongside her other A-levels, in business studies and economics. It meant she'd gone through a phase in her second year of sixth form when she'd taken photos of everyone and everything, and had put together a series of albums. She hadn't dreamt her mum would still have them, though.

"It's one of yours, but this isn't just any one. This is Jamie's album!" Sara laughed and wagged her finger at her little sister. "You should just be glad Dad never saw this when you were dating Jamie first time round, or he'd have run him out of town."

"He did that for himself." It didn't really hurt to talk about it anymore, but Anna didn't want to dwell on it, either. Otherwise, there was a chance she'd talk herself out of getting involved with him again.

"Sorry." Sara shook her head. "But you've got to look at this to see what I mean!"

She opened the album to the middle, where there was a double-page photo spread of Anna and Jamie kissing.

"I swear I invented the selfie!" Anna picked up the album and smiled at the images. Only a teenager could have put something like that together. "We took all of these ourselves, by turning the camera round and taking a photo while we were kissing. We used to spend most of our time doing that."

"Taking pictures, or kissing?"

"Both." Anna flicked through the album.

There were more photos, thankfully not all posed kissing shots. There were pictures of days out they'd had on the beach, and the time they'd snuck up to London for a weekend, both pretending to their parents that they were staying with friends. There were cinema ticket stubs, too, and even some dried flowers from a bunch of roses he'd bought her, pressed between the pages. She'd put the album together at the end of the summer, probably only a week, or two, before he'd left. It was a miracle it hadn't ended up on the bonfire, with the birthday and Christmas presents he'd bought her, and the sweatshirt he'd left behind. God, she'd hate to be a teenager again, experiencing all those intense feelings, with a heart that was so easy to break first time around and had never been quite the same since. No-one had understood how devastated she'd been. Even Sara had more, or less, told her she'd get over it, but then, she'd probably felt the problems she'd faced herself, at the same age, had been much more serious.

"What about now, are things progressing between you two?" Sara grinned. "Oh, come on, I've been married forever. At least let me have a bit of vicarious excitement!"

"I stopped taking photographs a long time ago." Despite her evasive reply, Anna was pretty sure the expression on her face gave her away.

"Say no more! I'm glad you're giving him a second chance. I didn't think you would."

"Neither did I. In fact, I didn't even mean to."

"Have you thought any more about what you're going to do after Christmas? Do you think you'll stay, now that things between you and Jamie have changed?" Sara put a hand on her arm. "I'd like him even more if you did."

"I thought a kid sister's job was to be annoying, and you'd want rid of me sooner, rather than later?"

"You were never that good at being annoying, and I missed you when you hardly ever came home."

"I missed you, too, and I'd like to stay, but it depends on where I can find work. One thing I know for sure, is that I've got to get out of here. I love Mum and Dad, but I just can't live with them."

"You can always stay with me and Joe, if you need to."

"Thank you."

Anna would never take up Sara's offer, but knowing she had her sister's unconditional support was more than enough. Not everyone had that, and it was why she was determined to raise as much money for Flashlight as she could. She wasn't even sure Jamie had ever had that sort of unconditional support. His relationship with Giles and Hugo had always looked odd from the outside, but she'd been too young first time around to count her own blessings. As an adult, she knew better, and it was a big part of the reason she'd been able to forgive Jamie much more quickly than she'd expected to.

"Well, you know the offer's always there." Sara took some cutlery out of one of the kitchen drawers. "So, are you all ready for tomorrow?"

"I think so." Anna got two plates out of the cupboard and put them on the kitchen table. "I just hope there aren't any more attempts to sabotage things. The choir's got the chance to raise a lot of money tomorrow, and quite a few of the other stalls are donating a percentage of their takings to Flashlight, too, so I'd hate for anything to go wrong."

It was the night before the Christmas fayre up at Harrington Hall, the first big event Anna had overseen, as well as the first official outing for the choir. Bethany, Mollie, Anna and Nancy had done some carol singing around the Bay, to help build up Mollie's confidence for her solo, and had already raised almost two-hundred pounds. But it had only involved singing in front of a few people at a time, and Mollie had told them she was having trouble sleeping, at the thought of performing to a big crowd, so Nancy was on standby to step in, on the off chance that Mollie couldn't face it on the day.

"Wow, who'd have thought Harrington Hall could give *EastEnders* a run for its money!" Sara uncorked the bottle of Prosecco she'd brought over with her. "Do you really think that Monica was the one who crashed the computer system just to get revenge for her friend?"

"I'm pretty sure it was her, but I'm not sure getting revenge for Christina was her motivation. Emily, the housekeeper I told you about, said Giles actually dumped Monica for Christina in the first place. So I think she's after her own revenge."

"Are you sure Emily isn't in on it? You know it's always the friendly ones you need to watch." Sara tipped her head to one side as she filled up Anna's glass. "Keep your friends close, but your enemies closer, and all that."

"You've been watching too many episodes of *Midsomer Murders*." Anna watched the bubbles rising to the top of her glass. "Anyway, have you ever seen Jean-Claude, Emily's husband?"

"He's got the French restaurant down by the harbour, hasn't he—where Nachos on the Bay used to be?"

"That's the one." She and Jamie were planning to go, as soon as they could fit it in.

"He's gorgeous!"

"Not just that, he's lovely, too. So I can't imagine Emily being remotely interested in Giles."

"Well, fingers crossed, nothing happens to put Mollie off performing. She definitely doesn't need to have her confidence knocked."

"We might have other problems if Patsy can't be civil to John."

"Do you think there's *any* chance he had something to do with his wife drowning?" Sara took a sip of her wine, and Anna shook her head.

"If the police investigation decided it was an accident, that's enough for me. And even if wasn't an accident, I'm sure John wasn't involved."

"What makes you so sure? There was a lot of talk at the time, about her seeing someone on the side."

"I don't know. It's just a gut feeling I suppose. Just because someone cheats on you, it doesn't necessarily make you capable of murder. Even if the rumours were true, and there was someone else, you know what the gossip in the Bay can be like."

"Oh, I know only too well, but can you really spot a bad 'un just by instinct?"

"Put it this way, I knew what sort of man Giles was the first time I met him, and he seems to fool plenty of other women. But even he's more complicated than he seems."

"Hmmm, I'll take your word for that." Sara was already topping up her glass, making the most of a night where she didn't have uni the next day. "Do you ever wonder how two brothers could end up being so different?"

"All the time."

Anna tried to ignore the feeling that had been nagging at her for days: that there was something Jamie wasn't telling her about why he'd left. If there'd been someone else back then, she'd rather just know. It was his honesty that set him apart from Giles, more than anything else. So if he was lying to her, it would be a deal breaker all over again, and this time there'd be no second chance.

****

Anna got to the Hall early on the morning of the Christmas fayre. Monica didn't work on Saturdays, so if she was going to cause problems, the damage would already have been done, but it seemed safer to have more time to prepare, just in case. Although, Anna and Emily had spent the day before ringing around the suppliers and stallholders, to make sure nothing had been cancelled and there wouldn't be any unwanted surprises.

Anna greeted Emily, as she met her in the main entrance hall. "It smells fabulous in here."

The scent of cinnamon and ginger that had filled the Hall on the first morning she'd met with Giles still lingered in the air, but there was also a hint of pine and mulled wine. The kitchen had apparently been cooking Christmas cookies for their onsite restaurant, since the very first of their Christmas events in November, and they'd added mulled wine to the menu for the fayre. Giles had arranged for another twenty Fraser firs to be delivered for the ballroom, where the stalls would be set up, and the aroma in there was like walking through a pine forest.

Anna had decorated the trees in an around-the-world theme, and she'd had less than two weeks from starting at the Hall to source the decorations: tiny paper lanterns from China, seashells and eucalyptus leaves on the Australian tree, and silk poinsettia flowers on the Spanish-themed tree. It had taken a lot of time, even when she hadn't been up at the Hall and hadn't been officially working, to theme all twenty trees. It looked really effective, though, and Anna allowed herself five minutes of satisfaction, as she followed Emily in to check that everything was ready for the stallholders.

"So, are you nervous about singing later?" Emily shifted one of the tables slightly to the right as she spoke, exactly as Anna would have done if she'd got there first. Emily was so easy to work with, and they seemed to instinctively think on the same wavelength. She'd been right that Monica would be the most difficult to deal with, too.

Unresponsive to Anna's suggestions, Monica took every opportunity she could to try and undermine her. Fortunately, the rest of the team had either been amenable from the start, or had come on board in the two weeks since Anna had been at the Hall. It had even been tempting to consider the offer Giles had made every other day since then, to take a permanent post once her gardening leave was over. Except, she needed something else, something more.

She just wished she was closer to figuring out what that was.

"I'm not nervous, but then I'll just be in the background. I could probably get away with miming, if I need to!"

Anna wondered how Mollie was feeling. She'd texted her before leaving home, to try and give her another confidence boost, but it was in the back of her mind that Mollie might duck out of her solo at the last minute. Nancy could stand in for her, but it wouldn't be the same.

"Do you want me to put a couple of the Flashlight collection boxes on the stalls, rather than all by the tree when you're performing? Just in case people are feeling generous with their change?"

"That would be great. Do you think we could get some of the staff to go around with the collecting tins, when we're singing, too?"

"No problem. I'll help, as well. Although, I should warn you that Giles has also asked me to take some photos of the choir for the website."

"Now I'm nervous!"

"You'll be fine."

She hadn't noticed Jamie come into the ballroom, but when Anna lifted her gaze, the nerves seemed to fade away. "You're here early." Reaching him, she kissed him very quickly on the lips. Although Emily was in the know about them dating again, Anna didn't particularly want Giles, or Hugo, to know, and Jamie didn't seem keen to tell them, either. So the Hall wasn't the place for any obvious displays of affection.

"I wanted to see if there was anything I could do to lend a hand." He looked around. "It looks great, though. I take it my brother isn't here, yet?"

"I haven't seen him." Emily smiled. "But it's always good to see you, Reverend Harrington."

"Jamie. How many times! Otherwise, I'm going to have to start calling you Mrs Dubois."

"Sorry, sorry, it's just a different rule for the rest of the family." Emily's cheeks coloured, and Jamie laughed.

"I hope by now you've realised I'm not a typical Harrington. At least, I hope not."

"I'm sorry again!" Emily laughed, too, but there were still two bright red spots on her cheeks. "I'm just going to make sure all my staff know what they should be doing, and see who wants to volunteer for the Flashlight collection later. I'll put some arms up backs, if I need to!"

"Thanks, Emily. See you in a bit." Anna watched her new friend leave, then turned towards Jamie. He smelled even better than the aroma of the Christmas cookies still drifting in from the kitchens.

"You look great." Jamie gave her a slow smile. "Christmas colours suit you."

"Thank you." She was wearing a red dress, with an oversized green and gold silk scarf draped around her neck, and she'd been worried she might look as if she was trying too hard. "So, what do you think of how it's all been set up? I haven't been here for years at Christmas, and I wanted to make sure I haven't let the usual standards slip."

"It's never looked as good, but then I always knew you'd do an amazing job." Jamie took hold of her hand. "I guess you're going to be pretty busy today, and we won't get a lot of time together?"

"I think you're right, especially as Giles is going to be around, and I'm sure your dad will come to the fayre at some point, too."

"Yeah, but probably only to act like this is all his doing." Jamie sighed. "I don't want to talk about him, though. Are you free to go for a drink, and maybe dinner, after the fayre?"

"Where were you thinking of? Do you want to go back to that pub again?"

"I thought we could have dinner at my place. I make a mean chicken curry, and it would be good to really talk."

"Sounds ominous."

"Not at all." He pulled her closer to him, kissing her again, and she had to force herself to pull away, despite the threat that Giles might turn up at any moment. "I just want us to have some time on our own."

"Well, if you're throwing in a chicken curry, how can I say no?" She let go of his hand, just as the first of the stallholders struggled in with an armful of Christmas wreaths.

Jamie rushed over to help the woman, and Anna tried to get her mind back on the job in hand. She wanted to be on her own with Jamie, too, but could she really give in to her feelings for him one-hundred percent, second time around? So far, she'd managed to hold on to a big enough part of her heart to protect herself from getting really hurt, if it all went wrong again. But she'd never been able to resist a good curry, and she wasn't doing very well at resisting Jamie, either.

She snuck another look in his direction as she headed across to tell a second stall holder where to set up, and at that exact moment he looked over at her and smiled.

Curry, or no curry, she was already lost. If Jamie Harrington broke her heart again, she didn't think it would ever recover.

****

The Christmas fayre was busier than Anna had dared hope it'd be. For the most part, the stalls had almost sold out by the time the choir were due to perform, and Giles had come over and thanked her for working so hard to make it a success. She'd also overheard a few people talking about the Christmas trees, and even her mum had seemed impressed, when she'd arrived with Sara and her teenage daughter, Jade.

Harrington Hall was far more beautiful than any office with a view of the Thames, and knowing there'd be a decent amount raised for Flashlight by the end of the day made it even better.

Anna had gone around and spoken to a few of the stallholders, whenever there'd been a chance between the almost relentless flow of customers. All of the collection boxes on the stalls had been really heavy—it seemed the spirit of the season was encouraging everyone to put their change in the pots.

Just before they were due to perform at four o'clock, Bethany and Mollie arrived with their mum and dad. Mollie's face was almost as pale as the snowflake pattern on her jumper. Her sister, by contrast, looked like she was more than ready to perform, and when Bethany opened up the big bag she was carrying, she pulled out a pair of reindeer antlers and put them on her head.

"I've brought all of our Christmas hats." As she spoke, she pulled out a green and red striped hat, with a large gold bell on the end. "Mum makes us wear one every year, and she's been collecting them for a while now. There are more than enough for everyone in the choir. What do you fancy being, a reindeer, Mrs Santa, an angel, or an elf?"

"I think in these colours I ought to be Mrs Santa, don't you?" Anna took the red and white hat Bethany passed her, which looked a bit like a red shower cap, trimmed with lace, with a sprig of holly stuck to the side. She was more determined than ever to hide at the back when Emily took the photos.

"Jamie's already taken the Santa hat, so it makes sense that you're Mrs Santa." Bethany gave her a knowing smile; she clearly didn't miss much. "What about you, Moll, what do you want to wear?"

"A paper bag, so no-one knows it's me, and I can't see if anyone laughs." The younger girl's hand shook as she reached out to take the fluffy halo made from a ring of white feathers, attached to a headband that Bethany had chosen for her.

"No-one's going to laugh at you. You're brilliant." Anna put a hand on Mollie's shoulder; it wasn't just her hands that were shaking. "But you know you don't have to do it, if you really don't want to, don't you?"

"I know, but I want to." Mollie voice was barely a whisper. "Except, Beth's invited her boyfriend, Tom, and some of his bandmates to come and watch us. I feel sick every time I think about it." If it was possible, even more colour drained out of her face.

"You've got it easy." Bethany pulled a face. "All you've got to do is sing. I've got to try and persuade poison Patsy to wear one of these hats!"

Anna couldn't help laughing. "That could be challenging." She should probably have pulled Bethany up for calling Patsy poisonous, but that would have made her a bit of hypocrite, given the nickname she and Sara had given their old neighbour growing up. "But you can't force her to do that, either. Let's just get through this first performance and hope Patsy and John can get past their differences."

"But she'll be the odd one out." Bethany was still at an age where that seemed like the end of the world.

"I think she probably likes it that way." Anna looked at her watch—it was almost time. "I'll go and find Jamie, and round the others up. I'm sure most of them will be willing to wear a hat. Are you sure you're going to be okay to sing the solo, Molly?"

"Un-huh." The poor girl could still hardly speak, but, hopefully, once she started singing, she'd forget her nerves. Maybe Nancy could give her some advice. She must have dealt with people who'd had stage fright in the past.

"I've just seen John, Nancy, and Jack come in on the other side of the ballroom, if you want to go and meet up with them? I'll send Sara over, and she can will deal with Patsy, if she turns up. Then I'll go and get Jamie, and meet you in a couple of minutes." If it was wrong to hope that Patsy might not show up, at all, Anna couldn't help it. But her hopes were dashed as she sent Sara over to the others, and she spotted Patsy pushing through a group of people gathered around a stall selling personalised wooden Christmas decorations.

"Planning to leave us in the lurch, are you?" Patsy looked Anna up and down, as she spoke. "And what on earth have you got on your head?"

"I'm Mrs Santa."

"You look more like Mrs Mop. I hope you're not expecting me to wear one of those!"

"Bethany's got the hats, and she's got plenty to choose from, but if you don't want to join in with the spirit of things, I don't think anyone will be that surprised." She hadn't planned to sink to Patsy's level, but there was only so much she could take.

Without waiting to hear the other woman's response, she left the ballroom in search of Jamie.

Crossing the entrance hall towards the staff area, which wasn't accessible to the public, she heard Giles's cultured tones. He didn't sound happy. Chances were, he was on the phone to one of his girlfriends, or maybe even Hugo, who thankfully hadn't shown up to spoil the atmosphere yet.

Feeling like the eavesdropper she was, Anna stopped outside the door of the office Giles was in. Just as she was about to knock, to see if he knew where Jamie was, she heard another voice.

"I just want to be straight with everyone," Jamie said. "I can't stand keeping it a secret anymore. It wasn't right to do it in the first place, but it feels even worse, now I know it's still having repercussions." Jamie's tone was calmer than his brother's, but he sounded resolute.

"And what exactly do you think that's going to achieve? It won't change what happened, will it? All it will do is cause more pain." Giles was getting louder and louder. "You've got so much to lose, never mind the rest of us. Do you really think it's more important to tell the truth, than to protect your own family from the fall out?"

"I'm a vicar, Giles. How can I stand up in church and preach about the importance of honesty, when I'm hiding this?" Jamie let out an audible sigh, and Anna raised her hand again to knock on the door, but she couldn't seem to do it.

"Just promise me you won't do anything silly today." Giles's tone softened. "At least give me the chance to speak to Dad first, see if I can find a way to limit the damage."

"I won't do anything today, but I'm not going to hold onto this secret forever, Giles. I just can't. We'll have to talk about this again later. I've got to go. The choir are due to start in five minutes, and you ought to get out there, too."

With no time to get out of Jamie's way, Anna wrapped her knuckles against the door. If she didn't want him to know she'd been eavesdropping, she'd have to pretend she'd only just got there.

Jamie almost knocked her over, as he flung open the door.

"Sorry, I was just getting a bit worried about where you'd got to." Anna tried to read the expression on his face. "We're due to start in a couple of minutes, so I thought I'd better come and find you. I hope I didn't interrupt anything."

"No, we were just talking about what to get Dad for Christmas, weren't we Jamie?" The lie tripped off Giles's tongue without him missing a beat, but he was well practised at lying.

What Anna hadn't expected was that Jamie would nod in response. He couldn't seem to look her in the eye. Whatever they'd been discussing, it wasn't what to get Hugo for Christmas. She just hoped he'd level with her when they were on their own later. Because if he didn't trust her with his secrets, then she wasn't sure she could trust him with her heart.

Chapter Nine

Jamie held his breath, as Mollie took centre stage. She was wearing an oversized pair of Elf ears, after Patsy had insisted the only hat she'd be willing to wear was the halo Mollie had been wearing. The teenager had handed it over with a smile, which had called Patsy's bluff, but worrying about a hat probably wasn't top of Mollie's priorities, anyway.

Nancy had given her a few techniques, and told her to fix her eyes on a point beyond the crowd and concentrate on that, so she could focus on the song and not be put off by making eye contact with anyone she knew.

They sang the first two carols as a group, but it was in the third song—*Oh, Holy Night*—that Mollie had her solo. It was a challenging melody, and the ballroom was absolutely packed, but when Molly started to sing, the silence from the crowd, contrasting with her voice as it rose up to the ceiling, made the hairs on the back of his neck stand up. The silence lasted for a few seconds after the carol had finished, before thunderous applause broke out, just as it had at the choir practice, and Mollie ducked out of view as quickly as she could.

"You were all amazing, but especially Mollie," Jamie said, as the applause finally died down.

Around them, the Hall's staff starting moving through the crowd, some of them handing out mulled wine and mince pies, and others shaking collection tins.

"See, I told you how good you were, Moll. I can't see Tom and Dylan, it's so crowded, but Tom's already texted to say you were sick." Bethany waved her mobile phone at her younger sister.

"That means good, right?" Jamie looked at Anna, who nodded. He wasn't even thirty, yet, but sometimes he felt older than time.

"I sort of enjoyed it in the end." Mollie managed a smile, at last. "And, hopefully, I won't feel so terrified next time."

"Is everyone okay for the tree lighting tomorrow?" Jamie turned towards Anna again.

She had a pensive look on her face, and he wanted to tell her how well he thought the fayre had gone, and that most of it was down to her, but it would have to wait until later.

"I think everyone has said they can make it already," Sara said.

Anna was still frowning. There was definitely something wrong.

"Oh, my God, that was sick!" A good-looking boy of about eighteen pushed in between him and Anna, and pulled Bethany into his arms, swinging her round and nearly sending Patsy sprawling into John.

"Do you mind?" Patsy shouted at the boy. "Didn't your parents teach you any manners, at all?"

He just gave her an apologetic shrug. "Sorry, but I had to tell Beth how good she was. And you." He turned towards Mollie. "You've got to promise me you'll think again about joining the band. If you can make a Christmas carol sound good, you can definitely sing swing, can't she, Dylan?" The boy tilted his head towards another lad, who'd come up behind him.

"I don't know if I can, Tom. I just about managed to get through it because I could hide in the middle of the choir. If I was singing in the band, I don't suppose you'd let me hide at the back, would you?"

"You're too good to hide at the back of anything." Dylan found his voice, and he looked at Mollie in a way Jamie recognised only too well.

The first time he'd seen Anna, he was sure he'd had that same look on his own face.

"Why don't we go into town and get a coffee, and we can talk about it. Dylan's already got an idea for an arrangement of some of our set that would be perfect for you." Bethany's boyfriend, Tom, put arm around her as he spoke, already leading her away.

Dylan and Mollie followed behind them, their hands so close they were almost touching.

"I think we better head off, too." Nancy glanced at Jack, who nodded.

"We've got to go and pick Toby up, and I think Nancy needs a rest before another big day tomorrow."

"I'll drive you both back," Sara said. "It's been a long day, and us midwives-to-be have got a duty to look after expectant mums!" She jangled her keys, as if to emphasise the point.

"Thank you." Nancy sighed. "I seem to move with all the speed of an arthritic tortoise these days."

"Are you sure you're okay for tomorrow?" Anna said, as Nancy rested a hand on her bump. The baby wasn't due until January, but even Jamie, who knew almost nothing about pregnancy, could see she was looking tired.

"I'm fine. I just need to sit down, before my ankles swell up to match my stomach." Nancy took Jack's arm, looking like she could use the support. "We'll see you at the tree lighting tomorrow. I just hope Toby can get some sleep tonight. It's the first time he's had any concept of Christmas, and even though he doesn't fully get it, yet, I can feel his excitement bubbling already."

"It must be great getting to live the excitement of Christmas all over again through him." Anna smiled. "Get some rest, and we'll see you tomorrow. But if you don't feel up to it, you've got to promise you'll say. Otherwise, you'll have Sara to answer to."

"I'll be fine, but I promise." Nancy and Jack headed towards the door of the ballroom, with Sara marching on ahead as if to part the way, even though the crowd had already thinned out a lot.

There were only twenty minutes of the fayre left, and Jamie could hear Patsy bargaining with a stallholder, to the side of where he was standing, haggling for a discount on their last holly wreath. He didn't know whether John had left, or not, but if he had, he hadn't said goodbye. Either way, it was just Jamie and Anna left.

"Wasn't Mollie amazing?" Anna still had a worried look on her face, despite the performance going better than Jamie had dared hope.

"Yes, and you were all great. I felt like a bit of a fraud."

"What do you mean?" Her tone was sharp, but he couldn't work out what he'd said wrong. She'd been fine before the fayre.

"Just standing up there, pretending I'm making a difference as a choir master, when not one of you really needs my help." Maybe it was best to change the subject. He didn't think, for a moment, that Anna was the sort of person to envy attention being on Mollie. But, whatever it was, she was acting strangely, and he'd rather wait until they were away from the Hall to talk about it. "Did you see the way Dylan looked at Mollie? It reminded me of how I used to look at you."

"*Used* to?"

He couldn't seem to stop saying the wrong thing. "You know what I mean." Maybe it couldn't wait until later, after all. "Anna, is something wrong? Have I done something to upset you?"

"You and Giles, I ..." Anna's mouth was open, but the panicked shout that Jamie heard next didn't come from her.

"Someone's taken the money!" Emily rushed up behind him. "All of the collection tins from the stalls have gone. We've only got the ones the staff were using to collect from the crowd left."

"Oh, God, are you sure?" Anna looked more worried than ever.

"We've been searching for the last ten minutes, and they haven't been put in any of the offices. All the stallholders thought they'd just been collected by a member of staff. It was so busy just after the choir performance, that no-one saw who took them."

"We need to call the police." Jamie glanced around. Almost all of the customers had already left. "Emily can you do that? And let Giles know? The Hall must have insurance to cover this." He knew how much it meant to Anna, and Giles owed it to both of them to put things right, whoever was at fault.

"You know where they should start?" Patsy appeared beside him, and Jamie knew what she was going to say. "With known criminals. Funny that no-one's seen John Casey since the end of the performance."

"For Heaven's sake, Patsy. For a start, John's never even been charged with a crime, as far and I know, never mind convicted, and he's more committed to raising money for Flashlight than any of us." Anna's eyes blazed.

With just a few words, Jamie could have put a stop to the accusations, once and for all, but he couldn't forget what Giles had said, either. It wasn't just about him.

"I don't want to hear anybody being accused. We've got CCTV, and the police will sort it out, but there's no way John's involved." Jamie put an arm around Anna, and he could feel her shaking.

She'd worked so hard to make the fayre a success and raise money for Flashlight. Whether the insurance covered it, or not, he'd make sure Giles paid up so the charity didn't miss out.

As his brother had pointed out, he had a pretty big bargaining chip. If Giles wanted him to keep the secret buried, then he'd have to pay. One way, or another, everyone would have to pay in the end.

****

"I'm sorry, this isn't what I intended when I invited you over for a curry." Jamie looked across at Anna after he'd ended the call. She was pretty sure it had been from Giles but she hadn't been able to pick up on all of the conversation. Jamie had still been on the phone when the takeaway turned up, so she'd answered the door. It was getting cold enough for snow, and the grass outside Jamie's cottage was already sparkling with frost. Winter was getting its grip on St Nicholas Bay. The lights on Jamie's Christmas tree gave the room a cosy glow, though, and it would have been perfect, if she hadn't been so worried about the money being stolen up at the Hall.

"It's fine. I don't think anyone saw today going the way it did." Anna passed the bag to Jamie and forced a smile. "I take it that was Giles?"

"Yes, and there's good news, and bad." Jamie put the containers of curry onto the warming plate as he spoke. "He's promised to double what was in the five collection tins that didn't get taken, and hopefully that will make up for the five that were stolen."

"And the bad news?"

"There's no CCTV. There's some issue with the system, and no-one seems to know how it happened. Although, I think the mystery about who took the tins is solved, even if the police don't think they'll be able to prove it."

"Who was it?" Anna's stomach turned over. The thought of anyone stealing from people in such desperate circumstances made her sick.

"It turns out that Monica sent in an email saying she won't be coming back, and that she couldn't stand working for ..." Jamie paused for a moment and shook his head. "Well, let's just say, she didn't describe Giles in the most glowing of terms. Apparently, she was at the fayre, too, but it was so busy, hardly anyone noticed she was there. Emily said she didn't see her."

"I know we thought it might be her who deleted all the meet-and-greet records, but just because she hates Giles and she's leaving, it doesn't mean she stole the tins. Giles had nothing to do with the fundraising."

"Yes, but it affects the reputation of the Hall and people thinking it's a safe place to visit. Apparently, Andy, the admin assistant Monica was training, told Emily some things that convinced her it was Monica, and she's passed the information on to the police. Her brother's a sergeant at the station in the Bay, so they're being quite open about how useful it's likely to be in making an arrest."

"What did Andy say?" Anna couldn't shift the feeling of dread, despite Giles's promise to match the money. She still hadn't had a chance to speak to Jamie about the argument she'd overheard him having with Giles, and she wouldn't be able to shake the feeling until she did.

"He was really upset about what had happened, and he's terrified he might lose his job." Jamie sighed. "Apparently, he saw Monica deleting the records from the database, but she said she'd go out with him if he didn't tell anyone. He also saw her at the fayre, bundled up in a hat and scarf, and she made him promise not to tell anyone she was there. But when the money disappeared, he couldn't keep quiet."

"Poor Andy. It was pretty obvious to all of us that he had a crush on Monica, and she clearly knew how to manipulate it."

"Aren't you angry? Giles said he'll leave you to decide what happens to him."

"He would, wouldn't he?"

Giles was something else, leaving the dirty work to her, when it all stemmed from his mess in the first place. No wonder he'd wanted her to take the job.

"I'm not angry with Andy. He was just protecting someone he had feelings for, who'd made him believe she felt the same. It wasn't like he was directly involved in deleting the database, or stealing the money. Does Emily's brother think the police can do *anything*?"

"They'll send someone down to speak to her, but without any CCTV, or witnesses to the actual theft, it's all just hearsay. At least Monica's left the Hall, so she can't do any more damage."

"Let's hope not. The thought that she could get away with stealing that money makes me so angry, though."

"I know, but you've got to try and let it go. The police will deal with it, if they can." He put his hand under her chin and tilted her face up. "You seemed on edge even before the money went missing. Have I done something to upset you?"

"No, it's just ..." It was no good. She'd have to have to admit to listening into their conversation. Otherwise, she'd only convince herself there was something serious that Jamie was keeping from her. "I heard you arguing with Giles."

"When?"

"I was coming to get you, to let you know the choir was about to start, and I heard raised voices. I didn't want to interrupt, so I waited for a minute, and I'd just knocked when you came charging out."

"What exactly did you hear?" There was no accusation in his tone. If he realised she'd stood and listened on purpose, he didn't seem to mind.

"Just Giles trying to persuade you not to say something." She really didn't want to doubt him, but he had a track record for keeping secrets. It turned out forgiving his sudden disappearance was a lot easier than forgetting it. If he wasn't honest with her, what was to stop him suddenly opting out of their relationship without warning again?

"I'm sorry, I should have told you what was going on with Giles." He pulled out one of the dining room chairs for her. "Will you sit down, so we can talk about it?"

"Now I'm really worried."

"You don't need to be. It's nothing you don't already know. At least, most of it." He poured her a glass of wine. "It's just, what you said before, about protecting someone you care about."

"Go on."

"Obviously, you know all about Giles and the problems his relationships with female staff up at the Hall have been causing?"

"I think today was evidence enough, don't you?"

"Exactly. It's got to a point where it's getting ridiculous. Except, Giles is desperate for Dad not to know what's behind the things that keep going wrong."

"So, it's a choice of protecting your brother, or being honest with your dad?" It didn't seem like that much of a dilemma to her. Giles could be a bit of an idiot, and he certainly didn't treat his girlfriends very well, but he wasn't a bad person at heart. As for Hugo, Anna wouldn't lose any sleep about lying to him.

"It's not just that." Jamie filled up his own glass. "It's some of the things that Giles has done ... It feels wrong, in my position, to be condoning them by keeping quiet about them."

"As a vicar, you mean?"

"Yes." Jamie looked at her again, but he didn't say anything for what felt like an eternity. "I found out that Christina, the events director before you, left her husband and baby daughter because she thought Giles meant the things he said to her. But it turns out he was seeing Monica at the same time. If I stand by and let him carry on like that, without making him face up to Dad and the consequences of his actions, does that make me any better than him?"

"Just because you know about something, it doesn't make you the guilty party."

"Doesn't it?"

"Can't you give Giles the opportunity to put it right and do something to make amends, rather than just telling your dad?"

"I already have. I've told him he's got to make a very generous donation to Flashlight, on top of matching the missing money, and that this is his last chance. I can't cover up for him forever." Jamie took her hand. "I just wish there weren't all these things going on at the moment. Having you back in my life is the best thing that's happened to me in years, but it's like there's a cloud hanging over everything."

"Only if we let it." Anna felt better already. She'd been so certain Jamie was hiding something from her, and knowing he wasn't, she was determined not to let Giles, or anyone else, ruin things. "That's one of the things I like best about you, that you always want to do the right thing."

"I do, but sometimes it isn't easy."

"And sometimes it is." Pressing her lips against his, Anna was certain it was the right thing to do—for once, it was just about the two of them.

Sadly, it didn't stay that way for long.

Chapter Ten

"It's snowing!" Bethany stuck out her tongue to catch a snowflake.

"Just as well we're so warmly dressed, then." Nancy looked at Anna and laughed.

"Are you trying to convince us, or yourself, that this was a good idea?" Smoothing down the hooped skirt she was wearing, Anna smiled to herself. If her ex-colleagues from the law firm could see her, they wouldn't recognise her. In fact, she barely recognised herself.

She still wasn't sure how she'd ended up standing in the middle of the square by the harbour, wearing full Victorian dress, but she was happier than she'd been for a long time. Nancy had managed to persuade a friend who ran the wardrobe department at a local theatre to let her borrow some of the costumes they'd used for a run of *Oliver* the previous year. It was certainly a step-up from the Christmas hats the day before.

Jack had been sent off to pick them up early that morning, and everyone had agreed to get into the spirit of things and put the costumes on. Even Patsy had seemed happy about it, but then Nancy had sorted her out the perfect outfit, which clearly set her apart from the rest of the group as a member of the upper classes. All the women had bonnets, even Bethany and Mollie, who didn't look entirely delighted to be wearing them. Although, it was Sara who seemed the most put out.

"Well, I'm really glad I booked a hair appointment this morning. I'll have helmet hair for the next month after wearing this thing!"

"You look great." Anna couldn't help smiling again. Sara wasn't usually the type to wear a dress, let alone a tartan one, over a hooped petticoat, with a matching bodice and lace shawl. She looked like a tornado had picked up the stock from an Edinburgh Wool Mill and dropped it on top of her.

"And you look like you owe me a *big* favour!"

"This is not my doing." Anna nudged her sister. "This was Nancy's idea."

"Maybe, but I only offered to join the choir with you, to make sure you gave Jamie a chance." Sara smiled. "And I've got a feeling you'll be thanking me for *that* for a long time."

"Shh!" Anna looked around to see who else was listening, but the rest of the choir were busy talking, or on their phones, as they waited to kick off the tree lighting.

Sara just laughed. "Please don't tell me you think you're keeping it a secret? It's blindingly obvious from the way you look at each other, every time you're both in the room. I think even Mum and Dad have cottoned on to it now."

"No way, she'd have said something. You know what she's like. She wouldn't be able to help herself."

"She's been a bit better lately." Sara's eyes were shining. "Mrs Moyes from the Post Office asked me how my university course was going on Thursday. She said Mum had been in there, telling her how many babies I've helped deliver during my training. I was so shocked, I could hardly answer her."

"It's about time, and she should be proud of you. I know I am."

"I know, and you putting Mum straight almost certainly had something to do with it."

"It's probably because I'm such a big disappointment to her now, too. She's been on and on at me to accept a permanent job at the Hall, but it's just not what I want."

"Well, don't take it, then. You're not desperate for money, are you?" Sara frowned. "If you are, we can give you some money. You know Joe's nan died last year? They've finally sorted out the estate. She had a huge house in Windsor, and there's only him and his dad to split it between. We'll be able to clear my student loan, help the kids out with uni, pay off the mortgage, and still have a bit left over."

"I'm so pleased for you and, thanks, but money's not the issue. I'm still getting paid, and I saved a decent chunk while I was working, but it means a lot that you've offered. Especially when you deserve to use that money to enjoy yourselves. I'm sure that's what Joe's grandma would have wanted. You and Joe have worked hard enough over the years." Anna gave her a quick hug. "There might actually be something in the pipeline, but I doubt Mum will be that impressed."

"As long as you're happy, that's all that matters. Somewhere deep down, I'm sure Mum feels the same." Sara pulled a face. "She's just very good at hiding it."

The tree lighting ceremony was the official start of the Christmas celebrations in St Nicholas Bay. The town relied on tourism all year round, but as a place that was most famous for its connections with *A Christmas Carol*, December was the busiest month by far.

A lot of the businesses were Dickens-themed, but at Christmas, even the people who were usually a bit less enthusiastic about the town's literary connections got involved. It meant that the choir were far from being the only ones dressed in Victorian costumes. There was a parade starting after the choir had sung their first two carols, which moved through the streets of the town, with the Christmas lights overhead lighting-up as the parade passed underneath. It was too far to expect everyone to walk up to the big church on the clifftop, so there would be a blessing outside St Nicholas Chapel on the harbour, which was dedicated to the patron saint of sailors and had given the town its name.

Over the years, however, some of the shopkeepers had decided it would be a good idea to link the St Nicholas name with Santa Claus, and Anna had never known anywhere else that could do Christmas quite as well.

The Christmas tree in the harbour was over twenty feet tall, and decorated with rows and rows of white lights, and hundreds of little wooden sailing boats, which were supposed to bring good fortune to the town for the coming year. There were also decorations made by the children from St Nicholas Bay Primary School.

Kate, whose wedding day was approaching fast, led a group of children from her class to hang the final decorations on the tree. Her little boy, Charlie, who clearly didn't want to be parted from his mum, held on to her hand—looking adorable in a tweed waistcoat and oversized cap, which he kept pushing back with his other hand.

Another bare Christmas tree stood outside the chapel, which would be decorated later in the month with memorial stars. It ensured everyone could be included in the Christmas celebrations, even those who were no longer around.

The children from the primary school were the first to perform, and by the time they'd finished singing *Away in a Manger* and *Little Donkey*, Anna was starting to worry that they'd be a hard act to follow. Mollie was definitely more confident the second time around, but she was singing a chorus of *Silent Night* on her own, and the high notes could be pretty hard to hit. John was due to sing a solo, too, when they performed again after the tree lighting, at the end of the parade, but if he was nervous, he didn't show it. Given all he'd been through, it was hardly surprising that singing a solo didn't worry him.

Kate and Will, along with Sara's twins, had offered to go around with the collection tins after the tree lighting. There was no way they'd risk leaving a collection tin on the stall selling hot chocolate and roasted chestnuts again. It was a shame some people couldn't think of others, even at Christmas, but that was the way it was.

There wasn't quite the same silence there'd been at the Hall, when Mollie started to sing, but that didn't stop her. And the more she sang, the less the crowd chatted. At one point, a baby was crying, but even that stopped when Mollie hit the highest note, and the crowd started to cheer.

"Never mind the tree lighting, I think a star might have been born," Anna whispered to Sara, as they followed behind Jamie to take their place near the front of the parade. "I just can't get over how good Mollie is."

"I know, and she might never have realised it, if it wasn't for Jamie." Sara straightened her bonnet, which had slipped backwards, making the ribbons slide up under her chin. "Her mum asked if he could start the choir up again, to try and build up her confidence, because she was too shy to join Nancy's amateur dramatics group. They'd tried to persuade Reverend Johns, but he wouldn't stand up to Patsy. You should hold on to Jamie, you know, you're meant to be together."

"I didn't realise that's why he started the choir." Jamie kept surprising her. And even though Sara was getting ahead of herself, she hoped they'd prove her right in the end.

It certainly made the job offer she'd had from Flashlight all the more appealing.

They were looking for a new head of media and promotions, and the managing director had told her that her CV was a good fit. But more than that, her interest in the charity set her apart—the cause genuinely mattered to her.

Pulling her coat more tightly around her, as they headed up the hill towards the first set of Christmas lights, Anna's thoughts strayed to Dane, the young man who'd been living rough near her old office building. Was he somewhere out of the cold, now that the weather had turned? He'd changed her life, and she wished she could turn back the clock and do more for him. Maybe she could persuade Sara to have a day's shopping in London. It would give her the excuse to go back and see whether Dane had moved on. If he hadn't, she'd like to offer him some more help.

As the parade reached the first set of Christmas lights, they came on. The first three sets of lights depicted the three ghosts from *A Christmas Carol*, and Anna's mind drifted back to the year before, when she'd been so certain she knew what to do with her life. She'd even had a five-year plan mapped out, to progress to the next level of her career.

What a difference a year could make.

A few flakes of snow drifted on the air, as the parade wound its way back towards the harbour, and the float carrying one of the Harrington Hall Santa Claus's appeared from the coast road. Some of the staff—including Andy, who was desperate to make amends—were helping Santa to hand out small presents to local children from the Hall's gift shop. Giles hadn't been sure about the idea, but Anna would eat her bonnet if it didn't result in the last few places getting booked for the Santa meet-and-greets.

Jamie stood beside her, as she watched the children collecting their gifts. "The kids are loving this. It was a brilliant idea. We should do it every year."

"Every year?" As she spoke, he took her hand in his. Any attempt at keeping their relationship low-key seemed completely forgotten.

"You are staying in the Bay, aren't you? I know I don't have the right to ask, when I was the one who disappeared last time, but I promise I'm not going anywhere."

She hadn't planned to tell him about the job, but as the flurry of snowflakes started to gather pace, and there was a chance it might actually start to settle, it seemed too perfect a moment to let pass. "I've been offered a job in Canterbury."

"That's brilliant! What is it?"

"It's heading up media and promotions for Flashlight, the charity we've been collecting for."

"That's amazing, Anna. I'm so pleased for you." He looked like he wanted to say something else, but then the crowd let out another huge cheer, as the mayor announced the countdown to lighting up the Christmas tree.

It was five o'clock and already dark. Jamie kept hold of her hand as the countdown began, and it was another moment Anna wanted to freeze. The accompanying flurry of snow was so unexpected and it was like a Hollywood moment—almost too good to be true—as the tree lit up in perfect time with the end of the countdown.

Jamie stepped forward to perform the blessing outside the chapel, and John launched into a pitch-perfect solo of *God Rest Ye Merry Gentlemen*. It was brilliant. But if something seemed too good to be true, it usually was. And it turned out the tree lighting was no exception.

"Shame!" The shout sounded from near the front of the crowd, as John finished singing, and a tall grey-haired man pushed his way forward and shook his fist at Jamie. "So, you let murderers sing in your choir, do you, Reverend? You all disgust me!"

The whole crowd seemed to turn and look in his direction.

Anna put her hand on John's shoulder, and his body slumped in response.

Jamie stepped forward. "If you've got something to say, Richard, I don't think now is the time, or the place, with all these children around. And whatever issue you've got with me, you can leave John out of it." Jamie somehow managed to keep his tone level.

"John Casey *is* the issue. It's not enough that he murdered his wife and got away with it, dragging half the town into his mess, but now you've got him singing in your misfit choir, and we've got to stand here and pretend it's all right!" Richard's face was bright red, the veins in his neck visible. "Well, I'm not just going to stand and take it. Not after what he put me through because he wasn't man enough to confess."

"That's enough, Richard." Giles suddenly emerged from farther back in the crowd, with a couple of the groundsmen from the Hall close behind him.

Richard was still shouting, as they strong-armed him away from the harbour.

Anna just hoped they wouldn't take it too far. The Hall really didn't need any more potential for bad publicity.

"I think we should go to the pub." Sara broke the silence, and John gave a small nod.

The poor man was as white as the flurry of snow, which had ended as quickly as it had begun.

No-one spoke as they walked up the hill towards Fezziwig's, but Anna didn't miss the way people were looking at John. She had no idea who Richard was, but more than ever, she wished she'd been able to freeze the moment before he'd ruined everything. If she'd known it was the start of everything unravelling, though, she might have chosen to forget she'd ever let Jamie back into her life.

****

Jamie brought Sara's and Anna's drinks back to the table, the only members of the choir who'd stayed behind in Fezziwig's. John had stayed for one drink before making his excuses, promising them he was okay. The others all had plans, and they hadn't even asked Patsy. But Jamie had bumped into Emily at the bar and invited her to join them, too.

Anna took the drink he passed her. "We've got to do something about Patsy." Sitting next to the roaring log fire, her cheeks burned, but Jamie wasn't sure it was down to the heat.

Sara pulled a face. "I don't think there's anything we *can* do with Patsy, except ignore her."

"She's had enough warnings about the way she treats John, but she still had to get a dig in about what Richard Heck said."

Anna had clearly had enough of Patsy, and if Jamie was honest, she wasn't the only one.

He knew Richard Heck from way back, but Emily had given the others some background into who he was, when she'd sat down to join them. He'd been the estate manager up at the Hall, and had been called in for questioning over the death of John's wife, along with a lot of others, when the police were investigating the possibility that she was having an affair. He clearly still had an axe to grind, but Patsy's only excuse was her personality, and Anna was right, they couldn't keep letting it pass.

"So, what do you suggest we do?" Jamie knew what was coming, but he wasn't sure if he could go through with it.

"Kick her out." Sara was the one to say it, but Anna backed her up straight away.

"She's got to go, Jamie. Surely, you can see that?"

"I can, but John is insisting he doesn't want that. I think he knows she's lonely. She was so different when Barry was alive."

"But that's not John's fault!" Anna put down her drink with a bang, making it clear she meant it.

"I know, but maybe we should just give her one final warning."

"She's had half-a-dozen of those! I know it's your job to forgive people, but it's not mine, or anyone else's, in the choir. I honestly can't believe John really wants her there, either. Some things don't deserve to be forgiven, and continually accusing an innocent man of murder is one of them."

"He is innocent, too. The police are convinced of it." Emily leaned slightly forward in her chair. "My brother, Seth, said all the reports suggest it was an accidental drowning, and even if it wasn't, John's got a rock solid alibi for where he was that night. Only, he probably doesn't want to broadcast it, because it doesn't paint their marriage in an entirely good light, either."

"Ooh, really! Can you tell us?" Sara tilted her ear towards Emily.

"I don't know all the details, and if I tell you, it didn't come from me, okay?" Emily looked furtively around her, as if the secret service might suddenly spring out from underneath the pine table they'd huddled round.

"I'm not sure we should be gossiping about this." Jamie had to say something, but when the others ignored him, he couldn't bring himself to turn away.

"I think most people know their marriage was going through a sticky patch. John was made redundant the year before Elizabeth died, and he took a job working in Manchester, which caused a bit of a rift between them. The night she died, he was up there, and he wasn't working ..."

"And ... Where was he?" Sara should have been a detective, or maybe a stand in for Jeremy Kyle.

"At his girlfriend's house in Salford."

"What if the girlfriend was just covering for him?" Sara was really getting into her stride.

Anna gave her a look. "You do know you're starting to sound like Patsy, don't you?"

"There were other witnesses, and CCTV, too, from an Indian restaurant in the town. He couldn't have been in the harbour. The autopsy report said Elizabeth had five times the legal drink drive limit of alcohol in her blood, and she almost certainly just fell, hit her head, and drowned. She couldn't swim, either."

"So, she was down there on her own? What about the younger boyfriend she was supposed to be seeing?" Sara had definitely missed her vocation, and Jamie was beginning to wish he'd made them stop talking about it. It was getting uncomfortable.

"They were never able to identify if that was true, let alone who it was. The CCTV camera at the harbour wasn't working." Emily took a sip of her drink.

"There seems to be a lot of that going on." Anna's eyes met Jamie's as she spoke.

"Hmm." Emily nodded. "Seth said it meant the police had to rely on the autopsy and the facts they *could* establish. One of which put John completely in the clear."

"So, why are people like Richard Heck so sure it was him?" Anna looked at Jamie, as if he had all the answers. If only it were that easy.

"It caused a lot of tension within families, when they called people in for questioning. Richard and John had got into an argument in a pub in Canterbury, the week before Elizabeth died. And Richard's son, Freddie, had to break it up. That put Richard in the frame as Elizabeth's secret boyfriend, and his wife nearly left him as result. I guess some people don't want John back as a reminder of all that." Emily shrugged. "I feel so sorry for him. It would be much easier for him, if Elizabeth's boyfriend just came forward, and everyone could put the final pieces of the puzzle together. Otherwise, I think some people won't ever believe he's innocent."

"No-one even knows for sure if there was a secret boyfriend!" Jamie's tone was more aggressive than he'd intended, but the topic had veered too close to home.

"But what we *do* know, for sure, is that it wasn't John." Anna seemed unable to let it go. "And someone needs to put Patsy right, once and for all."

A look of panic crossed Emily's face. "You can't tell her what I told you. She'd want to know where it came from, and it could get Seth into real trouble."

"I won't do that, but the autopsy results must be available to the public, surely? Maybe someone should start by sending her a copy of those." Anna frowned. "Or maybe a horse's head in the bed."

"She sees one of those, every time she looks in the mirror!" Sara laughed so hard at her own joke, she started to choke.

“I just wish there was something we could do to make things easier for John. It’s so unfair.” Even Sara’s joke didn’t seem to cheer Anna up.

“Sometimes, life just isn’t fair.” Jamie took a big swig of his drink. He needed another one.

Life wasn’t fair, and keeping a secret that could put John in the clear, once and for all, wasn’t fair, either.

Chapter Eleven

Anna had been right about organising the Santa float for the Christmas tree light-up. The Santa meet-and-greets were a complete sell out, and they'd even put on a couple of extra dates, to try and make sure no-one missed out. On the second Saturday in December—the day before Will and Kate's wedding—Anna had gone up to the Hall to get some feedback about the meet-and-greets, and to take some photos for the website.

"Seems to be going well, doesn't it?" Hugo sidled up to her, as she stood and watched a family group sitting with one of the Santas. "No doubt, that's got more to do with you than my useless son."

"Giles and I worked on it together." She wouldn't give him the satisfaction of telling him she'd found the final Santa, who'd turned out to be the best of all of them. Or that she'd had the idea for Mother Christmas's gingerbread shop, where the children waiting to see Santa could decorate gingerbread cookies. It was proving hugely popular, and had almost matched the revenue being made from the meet-and-greets themselves.

"If it's true, the changes must be the first good ideas he's had in years." Hugo put his hand on her arm. "Except hiring you, of course."

Anna shifted out of his grasp; he made her flesh crawl.

She'd never been more pleased to see Giles as he came over to join them. "We were just talking about you."

"All good, I hope?"

"Of course." Anna couldn't look him in the eye. "The feedback I've been getting from parents this morning has been amazing. When I checked Trip Advisor last night, we were the number one rated Christmas venue in the whole of Kent."

"*We*?" Giles smiled. "So, does that mean you're thinking about accepting my offer to stay on, after all?"

"I can't, Giles. I've loved it, but it just isn't right for me."

"Oh, come on, Giles. You don't think she'd really want to work with someone like you, do you?" Hugo was the most obnoxious person Anna had ever met. He even made her old boss seem charming.

"Actually, Giles has been great to work with." Anna could have said a lot more. But if her relationship with Jamie went anywhere, one way, or the other, she'd have to be civil to Hugo. So telling him what she thought of him wouldn't have been a good move.

Jamie walked over from where he'd been talking to some parents and stood next to Anna. "Not interrupting anything, am I?"

They were still struggling to get as much time together as she would have liked—it was his busiest time of year, after all. But it felt as if it was moving in the right direction, and taking a job locally meant she could look for somewhere nearby to live, too.

Her mum had calmed down a bit, and had finally accepted that Anna wouldn't be taking a job at the Hall, but Anna couldn't live back at home for much longer. They were used to their own space, as much as she was, and it turned out that seeing her parents kissing wasn't any less awkward at nearly thirty, than it had been when she was a teenager. It gave her hope, though, that after nearly forty years of marriage, her parents still wanted to hold hands and have a cuddle on the sofa.

She wanted that with Jamie. He'd said he didn't do casual relationships, and neither did she, when it came to him. There was a reason there'd never been anyone who'd compared in their time apart.

"You're not interrupting anything. I was just telling Lord Harrington how much I've enjoyed working for Giles." Anna saw the brothers exchange a look. They might not have been as close as she was with Sara, but they seemed to have developed a bond of sorts, lately, even if it was only a shared distance from their father.

"Everyone I spoke to today had nothing but good to say. Apparently, it's even better than previous years." Jamie smiled. "I'm going to do the reading of *A Christmas Carol* in a minute. That's if I can get any interest!"

"I'll come and listen to you." Anna could have listened to Jamie all day. He was a natural storyteller, and she'd seen what good use he put that to in his church services. So, when he'd offered to read a version of *A Christmas Carol* that had been re-written especially for children, Anna had signed him up for as many of the meet-and-greet sessions as he could fit in.

"Me, too." Giles was already moving towards the staircase.

They'd agreed to do the readings in the library, where there was another big Christmas tree that Anna had decorated with tiny replica books. Thankfully, Hugo didn't follow them. Muttering something about not wanting to waste his afternoon, he'd announced he was off to his gun club.

"Has your dad always been like that?" Anna might've been overstepping the mark, but Giles had the look of a beaten dog, as they positioned themselves in the corner of the library and waited for Jamie to start the story.

"What, an arsehole?"

"I was thinking bully, but that works, too."

"Like I've said to Jamie lots of times, I don't remember him being like it when mum was alive. I'm not sure if he was just happier then, or if she protected us."

"It must have been hard, losing your mum." It was the same conversation she'd had with Jamie before, but both men must have been affected, especially being left with a parent like Hugo.

"It was a difficult time. They discovered Dad had an aneurysm in his brain, not long after she died, and he had to have it clipped." Giles frowned. "Whether that changed dad's personality, I don't know, but I think Jamie and I got used to making allowances for his behaviour, and he got used to taking advantage of that."

"You and Jamie seem to be getting on better these days." It had been on the tip of her tongue to mention the argument she'd overheard, but she didn't know if Jamie had told him she knew, and she didn't want to rock the boat.

"We're very different people, but I've come to realise, since he's been back, that he's a better man than me."

"He is a good man, isn't he?" Anna stared across at Jamie, who was crouched down, talking to a little boy who seemed reluctant to let go of his mum's hand and take a seat on the rug for the story. Within seconds, he had the boy smiling, and the thought of what a good dad he'd make flashed through her head.

Now *she* was the one getting ahead of herself, but she'd never felt like this before.

"He is, and he told me about you two." Giles gave her a long look before he spoke again. "But no-one's perfect, not even Jamie. Promise me you'll remember that and give him a second chance, if he needs one?"

"I've already done that." She laughed, but a feeling of unease swept over her as Jamie started the story. Was there something Giles wasn't telling her?

****

Anna leaned into Jamie and he put his arm around her, as they left the library. "That was great. The question is, did you have as much fun reading it as we did listening to it?"

"The kids were really good." He'd nearly lost the thread of the story altogether, when he'd looked up and caught sight of Anna during the reading.

Seeing her there, in the library, where they'd spent so much time planning a future together, when they were barely more than kids themselves, had taken his breath away. She looked so beautiful, and she'd been watching him with such an intense look on her face. He'd known from the moment he saw her again that he still loved her, and he was certain she felt the same. If she knew the truth, though, she might feel differently. Could he risk telling her? He wanted to be honest with her, more than almost anything. The only thing he wanted more was to make sure she stayed in his life, and that was why he *couldn't* tell her. Living with his conscience was the price he'd have to pay.

"You're right, the kids were great. I couldn't believe they stayed quiet the whole time." Anna smiled. "It's almost made me sorry that I won't be running the Christmas events next year."

"We could always come back in a couple of years, as visitors."

"To the Christmas fayre?"

"I was thinking more about the Santa meet-and-greets." He paused as they headed back across the entrance hall.

"I think we're both a bit old to sit on Santa's knee." Despite the joke, she had a serious look on her face.

This wasn't where he'd plan to tell her how he felt, but life didn't follow a script, and he didn't want to wait for the perfect moment, in case it never came.

"I want to have kids, and I want to have them with someone I love. And I love you, Anna. If I'm honest, I always have, even when I ran away like an idiot without saying goodbye. I don't know if you feel the same, but I'm serious about us, and I thought it was only right to tell you now, in case you wanted to be the one to run."

"I do."

His heart lurched. "What?"

She wanted to run? Had he really got it that wrong?

"I feel the same. I love you, too." There was that look again, the one she'd given him in the library. Somehow he'd have to bury the thought that he didn't deserve her love, because he wanted it so much.

"Afternoon, Jamie, Anna." John Casey called to them from across the other side of the entrance hall. He was with a woman, with a noticeable baby bump, and a little boy of about two,

"Hi, John." Jamie shook his hand.

"I don't suppose you remember my daughter, Hayley, do you?" John introduced the woman next to him. "And this is my grandson, Alfie."

"Nice to see you again, Hayley." Jamie hadn't forgotten that John had a daughter, but he had wondered if they still spoke, or whether Elizabeth's death had driven a wedge between them. When John had said she couldn't make it home for Christmas, he'd wondered if that was a way of saving face. Seeing the two of them together was like a weight being lifted. It was turning out to be a very good day.

"And this is Anna. She helped set up the choir, and she's been really good to me, too." John smiled, as his daughter shook hands with Anna. They were both the right sort of age to have been at school with Hayley, but Anna and Jamie had gone to school out of the Bay.

"Thanks for helping Dad settle back in." Hayley looked at Anna and Jamie in turn. "I've wanted to move back to St Nicholas Bay since I had Alfie, and now that I'm expecting his little sister, I think the time is right. I had a good childhood here and lots of happy memories until ... until mum died. But I didn't want to come back unless Dad was here, too, so I'm really pleased he's doing things like joining the choir to help him settle in. My husband's in the army, and he's away a lot, so I need Dad to be close by."

"Can we persuade you to join the choir, too?" Anna got in first.

"I think I'm going to have my hands full, but if the house we've put an offer in on Dickens Lane is accepted, then we'll definitely be regulars at the Hall. Alfie can't wait to go and meet Santa." The little boy was already trying to pull his mum away.

"We better not hold you up, then." Jamie nodded his head towards the little boy and smiled. "And good luck with the house. See you at rehearsal, John."

John seemed to be getting his life back together, at last, so there was no need to rake up the past. Besides, it might do more harm than good. At least, that was what Jamie told himself. He just had to find a way to live with it.

Chapter Twelve

"Did you really do all this, Mum?" Anna studied the flowers again.

There were beautiful wreaths, in holly and ivy, strung with red satin ribbons down each of the windows on either side of the aisle, but the displays that had been made up especially for Will and Kate's wedding were even more stunning.

A beautiful spray hung over the gate into the churchyard, and another one in the porch. Louise had put hand-tied posies of holly, with red berries and white-berried mistletoe, on the end of every other pew, as well as two beautiful displays of seasonal flowers and deep red roses right by the aisle.

"I love doing it. Kate gave me a budget, and then just let me choose. She's been really easy-going. A lot of the brides I've done it for haven't been quite so relaxed. Some people have got very set ideas of what's right." She pulled a face, and Anna only just resisted the urge to laugh. Her mum could have been describing herself.

"I didn't even realise you'd done it for other brides." Anna looked at the display next to her. It was so beautifully done, as good as anything she'd seen in the high-end florists she'd occasionally treated herself to flowers from in London. Hand-tied with strips of hessian, they'd been beautiful, but nothing her mother couldn't outdo.

"I've been telling her for years that she ought to open her own shop. She's wasted doing cleaning, when she could be doing this." Anna's dad put an arm around her mum, but she shrugged him off.

"And I've been telling you for years that we can't afford to take the chance. It might be my lot in life to just be a cleaner, but at least it's always helped put food on the table and keep a roof over our heads."

"I wish you'd stop with that *just a cleaner* stuff, Mum." The more time Anna spent back in the Bay, the more she could see it. Her mother had a massive chip on her shoulder, for some reason. And it was why she acted the way she did, as if she had something to prove. "You worked up at the hospital for years, cleaning, and it kept people safe. Now you keep the church tidy, and help keep it running as a hub of the community. Not only that, but you go out and clean for people who can't do it themselves."

A lot of her mum's clients were elderly, and she also had a lady she cleaned for who was severely disabled. She hadn't put up her rate in years, and more often than not, she was late home because she'd done a shop for one of them, or taken them to the doctors.

"That's not how most people see it." Her mother shrugged.

"It's how *you* see it that matters, Mum." Anna gave her a hug. "And I'm proud of you. I always have been."

Jamie appeared at the head of the aisle. "The flowers look amazing, Louise. Your best yet."

As he walked towards them, Anna caught her breath. Vicars weren't usually the stuff of romantic fantasies, and Jamie's predecessor certainly hadn't been. Reverend Johns had the yellowest teeth Anna had ever seen, and halitosis that could fell a whole pew of parishioners if he came to too close. She'd never thought she'd find a dog collar sexy, or the black cassock Jamie wore, but somehow it emphasised how tall and broad shouldered he was. His sandy hair was just messy enough to be sexy, rather than scruffy, reminding her how much of his time he spent putting others first, instead of looking at himself in the mirror.

Thank God he'd told her he loved her. Otherwise, she'd have panicked about the strength of her feelings for him. Getting over him first time round had changed her forever, and she didn't even want to think about having to do it again.

"I just said exactly the same thing about the flowers." Anna smiled, and he stopped and kissed her very briefly, in the sort of way you could kiss someone in front of their parents. She felt it right down to her feet, all the same.

"I still can't believe you two are back together, or that you kept it from us for so long!" Her dad slapped Jamie on the back, and if that wasn't a sign of his approval, Anna didn't know what was.

When she'd told them the night before, they'd been surprised, but her mum had done a happy dance around the kitchen. Not that *her* approval had never been in doubt.

"Well, I can believe it!" Her mother nodded. "I always knew you two were made for each other, and Anna's always been a bit secretive. She didn't even tell us she'd decided to leave her job until she'd already done it, and now she's keeping us in the dark about what she's going to do next. Anyone would think she was being recruited by MI5."

Anna couldn't help laughing. Her mother would have loved that, but it would have been a disaster for national security. She'd have told everyone she met that her daughter was a spy, from the postmen to strangers in the bus queue. Just as well she'd agreed to take the job at Flashlight as soon as her gardening leave was up.

"At least I know who I can come to for wedding flowers!" Jamie laughed, but, when he looked back at her, Anna could tell it wasn't a joke.

Was that really where they were heading?

It was all moving so fast, and when Seb had so much as hinted about proposing, the thought had made her want to run until she dropped.

But with Jamie, she didn't want to run. All the stories she'd read, and all the people who'd told her she'd know when she'd met the right person, had been right. Jamie was it, and she wasn't afraid anymore, just thankful they'd found each other again, and that she hadn't let her pig-headed pride stop her from giving him another chance.

"I've got to go, but I'll see you after the services." He kissed her again. "Love you."

There, he'd said it again—in front of her mum and dad, too. That had to mean it was true, didn't it? And she had to believe he'd never hurt her again, either. At least until he proved her wrong.

****

The Christmas tree Hugo had donated had been decorated with strings of golden lights that led up towards a cross at the top. It was one of those dark, wintry days, where the light seemed to have completely faded by the time the wedding was due to start at three.

Anna, John, Patsy, Beth and Mollie weren't directly involved in the wedding, or the christening, so they'd taken their seats in the pews to the side of the altar that had traditionally been reserved for the choir.

Nancy, Jack and Sara would be joining them after they'd performed their duty as godparents.

Toby and Charlie made adorable page boys as they followed Will and his best man up the aisle, to wait for the bridal party. Whether Charlie would be quite so pleased about being splashed with water when he was christened was anyone's guess.

"I don't know if Alfie would be as good as those two, if he was here," John said to Anna, as she watched Jamie offering Will some last minute words of advice.

"He's so cute, though, and you must be really pleased you'll be getting a granddaughter soon, and that your daughter wants to settle back in the Bay."

"It was the reason I came back." John looked at her levelly. "When Elizabeth died, there was so much vicious gossip, I just wanted to get out."

"It must have been awful."

"It was. I don't know how much you know?" He held up his hand when she shook her head. "It's okay, I want to tell you. I'm sure you've heard enough to know that our marriage had hit a rocky patch? We were both looking for other things, but I was sure we'd get back to together eventually, and when she was killed ... the last thing I wanted to do was go to Salford and the woman I'd been seeing. I just wanted a second chance to put things right with Elizabeth, but it was something I could never have."

"So, what did you do?" Anna didn't want to push him, but if John was in the mood to talk, she wasn't going to stop him.

From the row behind, Anna could hear Patsy lecturing Bethany and Mollie about how much neater their hair would look if they tied it up, but John didn't seem worried whether they overheard, or not.

"I drifted," John looked up at the ceiling of the church for a moment. "Thank God Hayley never doubted me. She knew her mum and I were both far from perfect, and she didn't even seem to judge me for having the affair. Maybe because she'd have to judge Elizabeth, too, if she did, and neither of us wanted that. Hayley had her own life, though. She'd arranged to go off with her best friend to Australia for a gap year, and she went ahead with that. I think she wanted to get away from the Bay, as much as I did, and I knew when she got back, she'd go ahead with her plans to go to university in Bath, too. So there was nothing left for me here. Nothing but accusing looks and reminders of what I'd lost. Everywhere I looked, I saw Elizabeth, before things went wrong with her. I couldn't bear to look at the sea, knowing it had taken her life and I hadn't been there to save her."

"I'm so sorry. I hate that some people are still giving you a hard time." She glanced behind at Patsy, who was doing a very good job of pretending not to listen, even though Bethany and Mollie weren't being nearly so subtle.

"I thought I could deal with it, but when Richard Heck started on me ... I don't know." He gave her a small smile. "Thankfully, a lot of people, like you and most of the choir, have been great. I know most people are basically good, because I was saved by a stranger helping me out not long after it happened. It's the reason I volunteer at the soup kitchen, and why I'm so keen for us to help Flashlight."

"Were you living on the streets, then?"

"Not quite. I just abandoned our house here, and Hayley had to sort all that out from the other side of the world. I feel terrible now, about leaving that to her, but it would have been repossessed if she hadn't stepped in. One of her friends' parents had a relative who wanted to rent the house, and she set up an informal arrangement so it would cover the mortgage. It's thanks to Hayley that I've still got a house to come back to. I wasn't thinking straight at the time. I went to London, where I sofa-surfed for a bit with friends I had up there, but I didn't really want to be around anyone who knew Elizabeth and wanted to talk about what had happened. While I was there, I got a job and rented a bedsit, but I was drinking a lot, and I got sacked. I couldn't pay the rent, and ended up in a room in a hostel, but they had a limit on how long anyone could stay. There were just too many people who needed help, and not enough beds to go around."

"I know. I've realised how much of a need there is lately. It's like trying to bail out a boat with a thimble."

"I don't know what would have happened to me, if someone hadn't stepped in to sponsor me until I got back on my feet. I never found out who it was, but they organised it through the hostel, and arranged to pay for a bedsit for me until I found work. I ended up volunteering at the hostel, and the sponsor put me through my counselling training, and that's what I've been doing ever since. The hostel said that sponsorship was something that happened from time to time, but mostly the sponsors wanted anonymity. Whoever it was helped save my life, though."

"That's amazing."

It was what she wanted: to feel as if she'd made a difference to someone's life. She could see how much Jamie's work fulfilled him, too, and as the Wedding March started, and everyone else turned to look at Kate, she couldn't take her eyes off him. It was like the pieces of her life that hadn't seemed to fit together when she was in London had all, finally, fallen into place.

****

The wedding and christening went smoothly and even Charlie didn't make much fuss when Jamie baptised him. The choir had performed *Amazing Grace* during the signing of the register, and the personalised vows that Kate and Will exchanged had made Jamie's next words catch in his throat.

Whenever he'd looked up, he seemed to see Anna. If he'd been counting his blessings before she came back into his life, he didn't need to anymore. He could feel them every time he looked at her.

John Casey came and shook his hand, when Kate, Will, and the rest of the wedding party were posing for photos. "That was a beautiful service. Such a nice touch to combine the wedding with the christening."

"I can't really take credit for that. It was all Will and Kate's idea. The vows, too." Jamie smiled. "I think the choir contributed more than I did. That verse you and Mollie sang together at the end sounded amazing. I never knew there'd be so much talent in the Bay."

"Mollie's the real star." John returned his smile, but there were shadows on his face. "I'm just glad no-one heckled us this time."

"I'm sorry about Richard Heck, but if it helps, I think he'd been drinking. He'd probably have gone for someone else, if it hadn't been you."

"But I'll always be an easy target, won't I?" John was obviously tired. "I've been thinking more and more, since Hayley came to look at the house she wants to buy again, whether I should let her do it. Can I really let her move the kids here on the basis that I'll be around to help? Some people are always going to assume I'm guilty, and I don't want to be walking along the street with my grandchildren one day, and have someone shout out that their grandad's a murderer."

"It'll get better. Not everyone's like Patsy, or Richard."

"I know, but enough people are. And will it really get better? I couldn't sleep last night thinking about it, and I was talking to Anna earlier, about how I got back on the right path after my whole world fell apart. Getting out of the Bay saved me, and I don't want to end up running away again and leaving Hayley to pick up the pieces, like she had to at eighteen. It's not fair. It would be much better if I put a stop to it now, before she finalises the purchase of the house."

"I wish I could do something to make it easier for you." There was one thing Jamie could do, but the repercussions of it would be huge.

"Unfortunately, vicar, unless you can somehow convince everyone that Elizabeth's death had nothing to do with me, then I'll just have to thank you for listening." John shook his hand again. "You're a good man, Jamie, and I'm sorry I won't be able to stay on in the choir. Maybe you could just pray that Hayley can forgive me for letting her down all over again?"

As John finished speaking, there was a loud popping sound, and the lights on the Christmas tree suddenly died.

If Jamie had believed in signs, he'd have taken it as one, but he didn't need a sign. John had suffered enough, and Jamie would never be a good man until he spoke out.

He had to find Anna first, though. He'd been wanting to kiss her properly all day, and it might turn out to be his last chance. Because, once she found out what he'd done, he didn't think he'd ever get the chance to kiss her again. Whether he deserved it, or not, he wanted that memory of a perfect last kiss. It was more than John and Elizabeth had been given.

Chapter Thirteen

On the morning of the Christmas ball, all Anna thought she'd have to worry about was what to wear.

Giles had agreed to hold a silent auction of prizes that had been donated by local companies to raise more funds for Flashlight. But Jamie had been distant since the wedding. Not only had he been too busy to meet up all week, he wouldn't be going to the ball, either.

George padded across the hallway floor, meowing loudly as soon as Anna came down the stairs. Dishing up his breakfast, her stomach churned. The nagging feeling that history was about to repeat itself was getting worse.

Things had moved fast with Jamie, but he was the one who'd been driving it that way, and saying it was all, or nothing, for him. He couldn't just live with someone, he'd made that clear, and then there'd been the hints about getting married, and the fact he was the first to say *'I love you'* again. But, since the wedding, he'd been like a different person, and it was as if she could feel him pulling away from her all over again. She tried to convince herself he was just busy, but she couldn't shake the sense of dread.

Sara let herself in with the key she had to their parents' house. "Only me!"

Louise had gone out early, to make breakfast for one of her elderly clients who'd had a fall the week before, and their dad had gone to the fish market at Whitstable harbour, to pick up some oysters for Christmas. Anna couldn't stand them, but her mum had always insisted on having them, even though Anna wasn't sure her mother actually liked them herself. It was another case of keeping up with the neighbours that no-one, but Louise, even noticed.

Anna stood and filled the kettle. "You look worn out. Coffee?" She felt as tired as Sara looked. If Jamie was going to end things, she wished he'd just get on and do it. It was almost as bad waiting for it to happen.

"I had a shift at the hospital, and the last one was a bit of a tricky delivery, but they had a little girl in the end—nearly eleven pounds. They're going to call her Holly." Sara couldn't stop smiling, despite the fact she looked as though she was struggling to keep her eyes open.

"That's lovely."

"It is, but, Anna, you've just put six spoons of sugar in my cup. I know I look like I need it, but I'm not sure I can take quite that much glucose." Sara took the cup from her. "Are you alright?"

"Yes, no, I ..." She hated herself for the tears that sprung up so easily, but when Sara wrapped her arms around Anna, she just wanted her sister to be able to fix her problems—like she had when Anna was little.

"What's wrong?"

"I think Jamie's gearing up to leave again, or maybe just finish with me." She sniffed. "Sorry, I know it's stupid when other people have got real problems. But I really like him."

"*Like* him?" Sara leaned back and studied her. "It's obvious to anyone who looks at the two of you that you're in love. What makes you think he's going to end it?"

"I can feel him backing off. He's too busy to meet up—yes, I know it's a really busy time of year for him, but he doesn't sound the same when I talk to him, either. It's like he's trying to keep me at arm's length."

"Men get funny when they're trying to keep something secret, so they don't end up blurting it out by accident." Sara tapped the side of her nose. "You should have seen Joe when he was planning to propose. I convinced myself he was seeing someone else, and that he was going to walk out on me before the twins even arrived."

"Jamie's got form on that front. He left before, and I really don't think he's planning to propose."

"He was a teenager!" Sara let go of Anna's arms. "You can't keep doing this, Anna, wondering when he's going to leave again. And reading stuff into every little thing he does won't help with that. Otherwise, you'll never enjoy what you've got, and it might even drive him away for real in the end."

"It just feels so much like the last time." Anna stared down at George, who had finished his breakfast and was lying by the radiator, purring. At least one of the men in her life was easy to read. If George was well-fed and had a warm spot, or some sunshine, to lie in, he wouldn't be going anywhere. No wonder so many single women had a tendency to collect cats. They were much easier to understand than men. "You're right, though. I'm probably just being paranoid, and I don't want to talk about it anymore. I'd rather hear what's going on with you?"

"Good, just stop over-thinking it, okay? I actually popped in because I wanted to find out if you'd bought a Christmas present for Mum, yet?"

"No, why?" Anna had been Googling lists of *'what to buy for the person in your life who's impossible to buy for'* over the past couple of weeks, but she still hadn't thought of anything. If Sara had an idea, she was more than ready to hear it.

"Feel free to say no to this, and I don't know what money is like for you at the moment, but I was thinking we could club together and get Mum a flower studio for the back garden?"

"What's a flower studio?"

"One of Joe's mates manages a garden centre on the other side of Canterbury, and there's a franchise there that sells garden buildings—summer houses, playhouses, workshops, that sort of thing." Sara finished re-making the coffee as she spoke. "They're selling off some of the older display buildings really cheaply, to make way for some new stock in the spring, and he's given us first refusal on a big workshop that would make the perfect flower studio for Mum. It means she'd be able to start running a business from the back garden, and I think it should just about fit."

"That's a brilliant idea. I know it's only worrying about money and a lack of premises putting her off going for it. I hadn't realised until the wedding just how talented she is." Anna took the coffee Sara passed her.

"That's what I thought, and this way, she could start off on a smaller scale with no risk. Worst case scenario: they can use it as a summer house, or Dad will have somewhere else to spread his collection of power tools to! Have you seen my old room? It looks like the Black and Decker graveyard." Sara grinned. "And for once, with the money Joe inherited, I can afford to get everyone something decent. But if money's a bit tight for you, just put it what you can."

"I'm fine. I've hardly spent anything since I moved home, and I've been on full pay. Now I've got the job to go to at Flashlight, that's one thing I don't have to worry about."

"You don't have anything to worry about, Anna. So stop it!" Sara's words almost drowned out the sound of the doorbell, but not quite.

Ten minutes later, Anna would be wishing with all her heart that Sara had been right, but by then, it was too late and Jamie would be out of her life for good.

****

"It's a disaster, Anna. The band haven't shown up, and people are going to start arriving in half an hour." Emily was talking, but it was taking Anna's brain what felt like ages to process what was being said. As for it being a disaster, that was an overused word.

Putting her hand in her pocket and feeling the crumpled-up letter she'd stuffed there, Anna felt like she had more right to use it than Emily.

"Has someone phoned them?" Her words sounded slurred—not because she'd been drinking, but because her throat burned from crying. She'd already texted to tell Emily she was sick and wouldn't be able to make the ball. But Emily had phoned in a panic, and it looked like she was going to have to sort this out, too.

"Apparently, someone contacted them using Giles's email address, after he'd double checked that Christina hadn't already cancelled the band. They hacked into the system."

"Monica?"

"Looks like it. Turns out that, as well as stringing Andy along, she was seeing one of the IT guys, too. That's probably why the CCTV at the fayre didn't work. Either way, someone emailed the band's manager, paid them in full for the booking from the Hall's bank account, and said it was Giles's way of apologising for having to cancel, after all."

"Can't they perform now they know? Even if they're a bit late, it's better than nothing."

"They've booked another gig. I've tried ringing every local band listed on the internet, and it's no good. Everyone's already booked this time of year."

There was one person Anna could try, and if it stopped her having to go up to the Hall with eyes the colour of pickled beetroot, then it was worth a shot. There was also a good chance she'd run into Giles and Hugo if she went to the ball, and she couldn't be held accountable for her actions if she did.

It might not feel as if Christmas could get any worse, but spending the night in a police cell could just about top off the day she'd had so far.

"They're might be someone. I'll call you back as soon as I can."

****

It had been surprisingly easy to convince Mollie that the ball was the perfect time to finally take the plunge and sing in public with Tom's band. She'd agreed to start rehearsing with them, so they had a few songs she could sing, and a whole set they could perform without her.

Thank God they were an old-style swing band and not a death metal group, or the sound of silence would have been infinitely preferable.

She'd promised Mollie and Bethany that she'd try to get up to the Hall to see them perform if she could, but with her voice still not sounding like it belonged to her, they'd believed her when she'd said she might be too ill to go.

Lying on her bed an hour after the ball had started, she tried not to think about the piece of paper that was still stuffed in her pocket. But it was like it had taken on a life of its own, and she could feel it there, burning to be read again.

In the end, she couldn't resist it any longer, and she pulled out the letter that had been delivered with a huge bouquet of flowers, when Sara had answered the door. She'd screwed it up into a ball, but it was still readable, just about. It had been typed, but Jamie had signed it with his distinctive loopy signature. Otherwise, she could have tried to convince herself it was a hoax, written by Monica, or someone else with an axe to grind. As it was, there was no getting away from the truth, and all she wanted was to go back to a time when she hadn't known it.

My Darling Anna

I didn't want to write this letter, but it turns out that even after ten years, I'm no braver than I was before. This time it's not because I'm running away, but because I know you won't want to see me again when you read this letter, and coward that I am, I can't bear to see the look on your face when you do.

I've lied to you. I told you I left St Nicholas Bay to get away from my father, but that's only a very small part of the truth. I left because I discovered a secret that I was too cowardly, yet again, to reveal, and an innocent man suffered because of it. I never expected to see you or John Casey again, and I thought I could put it behind me, but the two of you coming back into my life has made me realise I can't hold onto this secret, no matter what the cost.

I know what happened to Elizabeth, and that's why I know for sure that John wasn't involved. She was seeing someone else, but it wasn't a younger man, it was my father. He was with her on the night she died, and although the police were right about it being accident, we'll never know for sure if he could have prevented it.

I thought keeping the secret was for the best at the time, but I couldn't live with it when John was driven out of the Bay. I had to go, too, and somehow try and make amends for my part in it all.

I thought finding my faith and making peace with God would be enough, but it isn't. At the wedding, I realised John would never have that sort of peace until he knew what had happened, but I also knew that telling the truth would mean I'd lose you all over again. I deserve the pain that's going to cause me, but you don't.

I love you, Anna. Always have, always will, but I know this is goodbye. I don't know if the police will charge me, Giles, or Dad, but I've already spoken to my bishop, and I want to leave the Bay, either way, as soon as possible. You've made a new life here, and you don't need me hanging around to ruin it.

I can't ask you to forgive me, when I don't forgive myself. All I want is for you to have the happy life you deserve.

I'm so sorry.

Jamie xx

Anna spent the next two hours watching cheesy Christmas movies, but she couldn't have recounted a single detail if her life had depended on it.

It was no good. She had to go up to the Hall and confront Giles and Hugo, and Jamie, if he was there. She'd thought about calling him, but unlike him, she wanted to be able to see his face, to look into his eyes when he answered the hundred, or so, questions she had for him, and judge for herself whether he was telling the truth.

He was right, though. She'd never be able to forgive him, much less trust him again. But she needed closure before she could even try and move on, and she had to speak to at least one of the Harringtons to get it.

George, who had been keeping her company, looked less than pleased to be turfed off the bed and shut back in the kitchen. Her eyes were still red rimmed, and she was dressed in jeans and a sweatshirt, rather than the cocktail dress she'd originally planned on wearing, but none of that mattered anymore. She had to get to the Hall.

She'd bought tickets for the ball for Sara, Joe, and her parents when she'd first started at the Hall, and Joe had driven them all up there. Sara was the only one who knew that Anna's sudden virus was a result of the letter from Jamie, and she'd promised not to breathe a word. It meant that Louise's car was still outside the cottage, so at least Anna wouldn't have to walk to the Hall on top of everything else.

"Anna! Are you feeling better?" Her mum was the last person she'd expected to see outside the staff entrance when she got out of the car. "And what on earth are you wearing?"

"I feel a bit better, but not well enough to go to the ball. I just needed to speak to Giles about something, and I didn't think I'd be able to get him on the phone. Sorry I didn't ask you about borrowing the car."

"Don't worry about that. I'm glad you're feeling better, love." Her mother had an animated look on her face. "It's all going on here!"

"What is?" Anna put a hand against the wall behind where her mum was standing, to steady herself. Maybe Sara hadn't been able to keep quiet about the letter, after all. Or maybe the police had turned up. That would send the St Nicholas Bay grapevine into overdrive.

"We got here at the same time as Nancy and her husband, and Sara noticed how swollen Nancy's ankles and face were. Nancy said she wasn't sure she was going to be able to stay, because she had such a bad headache and it was like she could see flashing lights." Her mother was almost dancing on the spot. "So Sara insisted on taking her and Jack to the hospital, to get her checked out. It turns out she had severe pre-eclampsia that sent her blood pressure through the roof, and if Sara hadn't spotted it, she might have had a stroke, or even lost the baby. But because of Sara, everything's going to be okay with them both. I'm so proud of her."

"Me, too." Anna felt a moment's relief from the relentless misery she'd felt since getting Jamie's letter. "And I'm so glad Nancy and the baby are going to be okay. But what are you doing out here?"

"I couldn't get a signal on my mobile to send a text indoors, so I came out here to do it."

"Who are you texting?"

"Just a few people to let them know what Sara's done. I can't believe I've got a daughter who's a lifesaver!"

"You've got every right to be proud." Some things never changed, but Sara deserved every bit of praise she got. "I'm going to find Giles, and then I'll probably head straight back home. By the way, what are the band like?"

"Brilliant. That young girl from your choir has a beautiful voice, but they're all good."

"That's great. Well, don't stay out here too long, Mum, and if you speak to Sara, tell her I think she's brilliant, too."

"I will, love." Her mother was already sending another text. She'd be dining out on this for months.

****

Anna eventually tracked down Giles in the library, nursing a large brandy. He didn't seem that surprised to see her.

"I need to talk to you." She didn't wait to be asked to sit down. She could have done with a brandy herself, but she wanted to get straight back in her car once she'd had it out with Giles.

"I thought you would." He looked across at her and sighed. "Jamie said he wrote you a letter explaining everything."

"I'm not sure it explained *everything*, because if it did, I still don't understand it. But he told me it was Hugo who was with Elizabeth on the night she died, and that you both knew about it and didn't tell anyone."

"I knew from the morning after it happened, but Jamie didn't find out until much later, when the autopsy report had already shown that Elizabeth's death was an accident. He overheard Dad and I arguing about it, but I still can't understand why he was so wrapped up in guilt about not going to the police. The investigation was already over by the time he found out."

"The investigation might have been over, but it still would have helped John and Hayley to know what really happened. It might have changed the police's view of things, too."

"Maybe, but I begged him not to tell anyone. I told him that it would kill Dad, with the health issues he's had. We've spent our lives edging around him and his moods, so we didn't make him stressed. It was emotional blackmail, I know, but it worked. Except, Jamie couldn't live with it, so he left not long afterwards."

"And what about the CCTV, was it you who had it wiped?"

"I didn't have anything to do with that, and Jamie certainly didn't, but I can't speak for Dad. He's always had a way of getting other people to do his dirty work for him. The reason everyone thought Elizabeth was seeing a younger man was because Dad got Richard Heck's son, Freddie, to do all the running around for him. He'd pick Elizabeth up and drive her to the Hall for their dates. Freddie used Richard's car without him knowing what for, and that's what put Richard in the frame, because Elizabeth was seen in his car. Of course, he denied it to the police and his wife, because he had no idea. It's why he was so angry, and why his marriage nearly ended over it. Jamie thinks we could have prevented that, too, but most of all, he hates what it's done to John and lying to someone he loves." His eyes met Anna's. "You."

"It's such a mess, but if it was an accident, I still don't understand why you couldn't just tell the police?"

"You know what it's like around here. Some people would have doubted it. But as much as he can be a really difficult man, I'm sure Dad didn't directly have anything to do with Elizabeth's death. He took her onto his boat that was moored in the harbour, and they shared a couple of bottles of champagne. He said they rowed, when she told him she wanted to make another go of it with John. He stormed off, and when he came back, he couldn't find her, but her shoes were still on the boat. He threw them overboard in a temper and got Freddie to pick him up and drive him home. But she must have fallen overboard, and that's what Jamie struggled with the most. The thought that she might still be alive, if Dad had checked, or raised the alarm with someone."

"I think he's right to struggle with that. You should, too, but especially your dad."

"None of this is Jamie's doing. Like I said, he didn't know until the case had been closed, and he was only eighteen. He listened to me, instead of his conscience, and he's paid the price ever since. But don't blame him, blame me."

"The thing is, Giles, I don't expect a lot from you, and even less from your dad, but Jamie ... That's what I find so hard. He just isn't the person I thought he was."

"I don't blame you for feeling that way about me, it's true. And, as for Dad, you certainly aren't the only person in the world, or even in this room, to feel that way about him. But I asked you to give Jamie a second chance if he needed it, and he's never needed it more."

"I just don't think I can, especially as he's doing it again—running away, instead of trusting me. That's no basis for a relationship, even when you don't take into account the lies he's told me." Anna felt exhausted by it all. The pieces of her life that had seemed to fall so neatly into place felt more shattered than ever. "What's going to happen, now that Jamie has gone to the police?"

"They're talking to Dad now, but our lawyer seems to think they won't be able to bring charges after all this time, although John and his daughter might want to sue for wrongful death. Either way, Jamie definitely isn't implicated in any way. If the police agree he's innocent, I think you should, too."

Anna stood up to leave. "I think we've established the police don't always know the full story, haven't we?"

Jamie had broken her trust again. Second chances were one thing, but giving him a third chance would just make her a fool.

Chapter Fourteen

Nancy and her baby daughter, Sarina, were both doing well. She'd been given the name as a thank you to Sara, and by the day before Christmas Eve, Louise must have told everyone she knew, as well as hundreds of people she didn't, that her daughter was a lifesaver.

Anna had finished at the Hall, thankfully. She'd miss Emily and some of the others, but the chance of bumping into Hugo and giving him a piece of her mind was a risk she could do without. She hadn't contacted Jamie, and he hadn't attempted to contact her again, either. The fact that Elizabeth had been having an affair with Hugo had filtered into the Bay's grapevine, once news of Hugo's questioning by the police had got out, which meant John had been vindicated, at last.

For about twenty-four hours after getting Jamie's letter, Anna had contemplated going back to London and the anonymity it provided. There'd be no chance of bumping into Jamie, or any of the other Harrington men. And there wouldn't be the constant reminders of what she and Jamie had shared, either.

She wouldn't, though. She might have allowed herself to think they could have a future, but why should she give up her dream job? The thought of starting work at Flashlight in the New Year was the one thing she had to look forward to.

She'd booked some appointments to view flats in Canterbury after Christmas, too. Before Jamie's revelations, she'd planned to rent somewhere in the Bay, but now she couldn't wait to get out.

Leaving George snuggled up on the Christmas edition of the *Radio Times*, which he seemed to prefer to his cat bed, Anna headed out for a walk along the beach. It was a blowy day, and she was hoping it could clear her head—it might even help her to sleep later on. Her parents had gone out with friends for lunch, and she hadn't wanted to tag along, even though they'd invited her. Being in the choir had made Anna feel like she belonged back in the Bay, and she'd started to build new friendships as a result, particularly with Nancy and John, and she'd grown closer to Sara again, too. Then there'd been her work at the Hall. Despite the issues with Monica, and the looming presence of Hugo, she'd become really friendly with Emily, and had even started to like Giles.

Now everything had fallen apart. The choir were hardly going to want to perform together, not after the way John must feel about Jamie and the rest of the Harringtons, and Anna intended to steer well clear of the Hall.

With Nancy set to stay in hospital over Christmas, and Sara busy with her own family, Anna found herself left at a loose end again, as if the months she'd spent trying to start over in the Bay had counted for nothing.

Canterbury would be a fresh start, though. She just had to get through the next few days, and then she could spend January getting the new flat straight. She wouldn't have so much time to think, then, and that had to make things easier, didn't it?

Walking along the sea wall towards the harbour, Anna stopped to look at the boats. Some of them had fairy-lights, and one even had a full-sized Christmas tree on its deck. She'd almost forgotten that Christmas was only two days away. It definitely didn't feel like it anymore.

"Anna!"

She braced herself to duck behind one of the brick-built beach huts—if it was Jamie, she didn't want to speak to him—but, glancing up, she realised it was John, one of the few people she *was* happy to see.

"How are you?" She walked towards him, sagging with relief when he gave her a hug. She'd thought she might have to explain that she hadn't known Jamie's secret, but she could tell by his face there was no explanation needed.

"I'm fine. I've just been into town. I realised I didn't have any sage and onion stuffing, and I didn't want to leave it until tomorrow."

"I thought you were working in the soup kitchen on Christmas day?"

"I'm doing the lunchtime session, but I've got company in the evening, so I thought I'd better do something other than cheese on toast!" John laughed.

"Are Hayley and Alfie coming, after all?"

"No, they're going to Hayley's in-laws, and then coming to me the day after Boxing Day, until after New Year. But you're never going to guess who is coming for dinner."

"Oh, I don't know, Santa Claus, Shergar, Lord Lucan?" Anna could barely think straight, as it was.

"Patsy Bell!"

"I hope you've got a bodyguard." She looked around quickly, wondering if there was a bench she could sit on before she fell down. The world really had gone mad. "I take it she's finally seen sense, now that everyone knows it was Hugo with Elizabeth on the night she died."

"Actually, she asked me before that, after the wedding." John furrowed his brow. "Whether she overheard us talking, or whether it was when I was telling Jamie I didn't think I'd ever be able to make a life in the Bay again, I don't know. But something must have hit home with her. She apologised and told me how lonely she'd been since Barry died, and that she knew what losing someone could do to a person. She admitted she sometimes lashes out at other people because of it, and then she asked me what I was doing on Christmas day."

"That's got to qualify as a Christmas miracle." Anna really would need to sit down, if this carried on.

"She's helping me at the soup kitchen, too."

"That's great, John, it really is. Although, I must say, I never expected a friendship between you two." Maybe some people really could change. "So, how are you feeling about staying in the Bay now?"

"Jamie's made it possible, and it's what Hayley really wants, too. I think next year's going to be a good one." There didn't seem to be a trace of bitterness in his voice when he mentioned Jamie, but she had to ask.

"Aren't you angry, that your name could have been cleared a long time ago?"

"I was never angry at Jamie, even when he first told me what he knew, and explained why he hadn't come forward. He was just a kid when it happened, and I know how badly his loyalties would have been split. He was the same age as Hayley, and she had to take the responsibility of sorting everything out when I went AWOL. So I know he would have done the same, to try and support his dad, especially as they were always so worried about his health." John frowned. "But I felt like killing Hugo and Giles. I went up to the Hall and confronted Giles. Predictably, Hugo had disappeared to stay with his cousin as soon as the police released him."

"What did Giles say?" Anna suspected she already knew the answer—probably the same as he'd said to her. There wasn't much else he could say.

"He told me he'd emotionally blackmailed Jamie, to convince him to keep quiet, and that Jamie hadn't known the truth until I'd already decided that I had to leave the Bay. I was really angry, too, because I'd convinced myself that Giles was my sponsor, and that he'd donated money to the hostel out of guilt. I couldn't believe I'd been grateful all this time, and it had just been blood money."

"What did he say about that?"

"He said it wasn't him, but he knew who it was. I've got to admit, I lost it then and pinned him up against the wall, because it would have been even worse to find out it was Hugo."

"And was it?"

"No, it was Jamie." John's eyes met hers. "And it wasn't like he did it with Harrington money, either, because Hugo cut off his allowance after he left. Giles said Jamie took two jobs when he started his training, so he could support himself and sponsor me. If I'd had even a shred of anger towards him, it would have melted away knowing that. He made sacrifices to try and put something right that wasn't even his mistake, and he's been putting other people first ever since. If anything good has come from this whole mess, it's the fact that Jamie has dedicated his life to helping others. But Sara tells me you don't want to see him anymore?"

"I don't trust him. I thought I was in love with him, but I didn't even really know who he was."

"We all make mistakes." John wiped his eyes with the back of his hand. "And I know better than anyone that we don't all get the chance to apologise, or to give things another go. I come down to the harbour, sometimes, to talk to Lizzie, now that I can finally look at the sea without losing it. But it's not the same as having the chance to actually talk to her, and to say that I'm sorry for not trying harder to sort out our marriage. I'd give anything to be forgiven and have the chance to forgive her for the mistakes she made. Don't blow that opportunity, Anna."

"I ..." She started, but she couldn't find the words to answer him.

"Happy Christmas, and promise me you'll make the next year count?" John gave her another quick hug, and she just managed to wish him a happy Christmas in return, before he disappeared out of view on the other side of the beach huts.

So much for clearing her head. The walk had given her more to think about than ever.

Chapter Fifteen

Anna's mother stood by the French windows and looked out at the pile of wooden sections that would eventually be her flower studio. "I still can't get over the fact that you girls have done this for me! I'm so lucky to have two such amazing daughters."

They'd had to have it delivered on Christmas Eve, as there'd been no way of getting it there on Christmas Day, and Louise had burst into tears when she'd discovered that her daughters had bought the building so she could start her dream business.

"I'm going to keep my older cleaning clients on, and the lady I help who's in a wheelchair, but I should be able to gradually reduce the other customers I clean for, as the business takes off. It feels like I've won the lottery."

"It was all Sara's idea." Anna looked up from the kitchen table, where she'd been nursing a cup of tea for the best part of half an hour, and smiled as her mum turned towards her. She really was like a kid on Christmas morning, who'd been given the toy at the very top of her list.

"It doesn't matter whose idea it was. I couldn't be prouder of the two of you, or the jobs you'll both be doing, once you start at Flashlight." Her mother headed over and put her arms around Anna. "I know I wasn't always the best at showing it, and it's taken me a long time to realise it, but it was only because I wanted the best for you, and I didn't want you to end up like me."

"I wouldn't mind ending up like you, Mum."

"Well, one thing I did do right was find a lovely supportive husband, who gave me two beautiful daughters." Her mother might not have mentioned Jamie, but it was obvious what she was getting at. "Are you sure you don't want to come to church with us?"

"No, I'm going to sit on the sofa with George and watch *It's A Wonderful Life*. If that doesn't finally give me a Christmassy feeling, then nothing will!"

"Okay, love. Well, we're going for a drink with Kate's parents after church, so we might not be back until late, but we'll be in Fezziwig's, if you want to join us."

"Thanks, but George and I will be fine at home."

"You ready, Lou?" her dad said, popping his head around the door to the kitchen, and delivering a powerful waft of his aftershave. "See you later, Anna."

"Bye, have fun!"

After her parents had left, Anna was true to her word. Opening a tin of Quality Street and pouring a glass of Bailey's, she tried to convince herself that this wasn't the most tragic Christmas Eve ever.

Over in his usual spot, George had stretched out on his back, with his paws above his head and his furry orange belly moving up and down in rhythm with his purring. At least one of them seemed to be having the perfect Christmas Eve.

She watched *It's a Wonderful Life* first, followed by *Love Actually*, but it could have been a wet Wednesday in the middle of March, for all the Christmas spirit she felt. The New Year couldn't come fast enough.

Desperate to take her mind off Jamie, she pulled the information pack from the envelope that Flashlight had sent the day before. She read through her contract again, and a leaflet about the charity's aims and objectives.

Flicking through the rest of the pack, she came to a fortnightly newsletter called *Inside*. There were various articles from people who'd been homeless and had managed to turn their lives around. Reading through the articles, Anna felt a tiny bit better. Even when people were at their lowest, there was always a chance that they could find a way back. So, surely, she should be able to get over Jamie?

The final section of the newsletter had photographs, emails and letters, from people sharing their stories about homelessness. Some of them were from people who'd lived on the streets, and some were from members of the public whose perceptions had been changed after they'd met a homeless person.

On the second to last page, she saw it: a photograph of someone she recognised. She had to look three times to be sure, but it really was Dane, the young homeless man she'd given money to on the day she'd decided to leave her job. In his email, Dane mentioned being given money by a stranger a couple of weeks earlier. He wrote about the stupid decisions he'd made as a teenager, and how, feeling like he couldn't face his family, he'd run away to London. The quote said he'd ended up on the streets and hadn't had the money, or courage, to go back to his family in Cornwall, to see if they could patch things up, but the money he'd been given by the stranger was enough for him to clean himself up and pay his train fare back to Truro, to take a chance on rebuilding a relationship with his mum. He'd admitted there were no guarantees things would work out, but getting a chance to try was all he could ask for. Like all good Christmas stories, Dane's had a happy ending, and he finished by saying how much he was looking forward to spending his first Christmas off the streets in two years, and his first with his family for five years.

The last line was almost an echo of what John had said on the beach, about everyone making mistakes, but not everyone having the chance to put them right.

With tears in her eyes, Anna pushed the information pack back in the envelope and looked at George. "Do you ever feel like the world is trying to tell you something?"

The cat blinked and stretched out again, taking up her place on the sofa, as well as his own.

"Okay, I get the message. You want me to go out and find Jamie, too, don't you?"

She looked at her watch. It was half-past ten, which meant midnight mass would be starting in an hour. She probably wouldn't have the chance to speak to him beforehand, but when she saw him at the service, she'd know whether or not talking to him would be the right thing to do.

****

An hour later, she sat at the end of a pew, on the second row from the back of the church.

When Reverend Johns had been in charge, all the Christmas services had been down at the chapel on the harbour, but since Jamie had arrived, more and more people had been attending the services, and so they were being held in the big church on the clifftop.

It was packed, and there was a noisy crowd across the aisle from her, who'd obviously decided to go to Midnight Mass on the way back from the pub. Jamie had his hands full managing them and trying to keep the service running.

That unmistakable Christmassy moment finally came for Anna, when the lights in the church dimmed and the whole congregation held up candles as they sang the last carol. She watched Jamie patiently helping an elderly couple re-light their candles for the third time, after the husband kept coughing and blowing them out, and his wife laughed every time. That was what she wanted—not a winter cough—but to be sitting side-by-side with someone in fifty years' time, being able to laugh even when things went wrong. But she didn't want that to be just anyone, she wanted it to be Jamie.

Things would go wrong, sometimes, and they'd both make mistakes, but love was about finding a way to forgive each other and get through all that. She wanted to make a life with Jamie and she wanted to make it in the Bay. She only hoped it wasn't too late.

Coming into church, she'd felt more of a sense of belonging than she'd had for as long as she could remember. Kate and Will, with Charlie asleep in his buggy, had been on their way in at the same time, and they'd exchanged Christmas greetings and plans to get together with Sara, Nancy and their husbands in the New Year.

Bethany and Mollie had been there with their parents, and had both come over to give Anna a Christmas hug, and to thank her for giving their band their first big gig. Mollie had the biggest grin on her face when she'd told Anna they already had two more bookings off the back of their performance at the Hall.

Even John and Patsy had been there, with her arm linked through his. When Patsy had let go of John and embraced Anna, too, she'd almost had to pinch herself to check she wasn't dreaming.

Whatever happened, she wouldn't be moving to Canterbury. Her life was in the Bay, and a half-hour commute to work was nothing in comparison to losing that sense of belonging.

She just needed one more Christmas miracle. She wanted Jamie to tell her he was staying in the Bay, too, and to forgive her for not knowing when to give him a chance to explain, or for understanding that the mistake he'd made had been with the best of intentions.

At the end of the service, it felt like the last of the congregation would never leave. Anna was trying hard to hold onto her Christmas spirit and be charitable, when some of the parishioners wanted to stay and chat after the service. After all, some of them would probably be spending Christmas day alone. It didn't help that when she caught Jamie's eye a couple of times, she couldn't read his expression. Was it already too late?

"Night, Vicar!"

When the final member of the congregation finally left, the cold night air caught in the back of Anna's throat, as Jamie closed the door to the church's porch, sliding the bolt upwards.

"I thought I was hallucinating when I looked up and saw you sitting at the end of that pew." He moved to stand in front of her, and she had to stop herself from just throwing her arms around his neck.

He had dark circles beneath his eyes, and his hair looked like he'd run his hands through it a hundred times, but he seemed more handsome than ever, and Anna realised she'd been right. She hadn't just known whether she wanted to talk to him once she'd seen him—she'd known how she felt, too. She loved him, and there wasn't a thing she could do about it, and even less that she wanted to.

"I'm sorry I didn't contact you after I got your letter." She dropped her gaze for a moment. "But there was a lot to take in."

"I didn't know if I'd ever see you again." He cupped a hand under her chin, as he'd done so many times before, so that she had to look at him. "And I'm the one who's sorry."

"Someone told me that everyone makes mistakes, but not everyone has a chance to put them right. I'm hoping that we've got that chance." It had sounded better in her head than it did when she said it out loud, but Jamie's smile suggested it was the right thing to say.

"I love you, Anna, and I'd like to spend the rest of my life putting the mistakes I've made right."

"But what about this?" She looked around the church. "I know you said you wanted to leave the Bay, but it's where we met, and where we fell in love. Twice. And I can't think of anywhere else I'd rather be."

"If you wanted me to move to the other side of the world, I'd do it to be with you. But you're right, and you're not the only one who thinks so." Jamie laughed, and it echoed around the empty church. "When I spoke to my bishop about wanting to move, she told me that the best way I could make up for my mistakes was to serve the community in which I'd made them. She also told me to wait and pray, before I made any hasty decisions, but all my prayers were for one thing."

"What was that?"

"For another chance with you."

"You don't need to waste your prayers on me, anymore, there are far more deserving causes." Anna stood on her tiptoes and tilted her head. "I love you, too, Jamie Harrington. Like you said, always have and always will, whatever mistakes we make along the way. Now, it's already over two hours into Christmas day. Are you going to kiss me, or do I have to wait for divine intervention for that, too?"

"I think I can manage that. Happy Christmas."

"Happy Christmas."

He kissed her gently, and she leant against him, knowing without a shred of doubt that she was home, in the Bay, but most of all in Jamie's arms, and she was never leaving again.

The End

Acknowledgements

My thanks go to my fellow authors and all at Fabrian books, as well as to my writing family – The Write Romantics. Also to Jennie at Dunwrite Authoring Services for her work on the final version of the book. Not forgetting Mollie and Bethany Johnson, who lent their names to two of the characters in this book.

Finally, to my husband and children, for being patient when I am glued to the laptop and not really listening to what you say – with thanks and much love.

Also available from this author

The Christmas Shop at Central Park

By Jo Bartlett

Libby Cooper hasn't celebrated Christmas for four years. How can she when the most important people in her life are no longer around to enjoy the festivities – because of her?

Hiding out in her grandparents' failing micro-pub, she wants to forget that the season of goodwill even exists; but her grandmother has other ideas. It's time for Libby to face her fears – and Christmas – head on. And what better way to immerse herself in the celebrations than working in her great aunt's Christmas shop, just three blocks from Central Park?

Making new friends is the easy bit, but leaving the past behind proves much more difficult. The only way Libby can cope is by taking long walks in Central Park and joining an art therapy group to help her express her emotions.

Harry Stanwick is a Central Park Ranger, who's as beautiful on the inside as he is on the outside. He seems to know instinctively when Libby wants to talk and when she just needs to be left alone.

Working with Harry and the rest of her new friends to save an old off-Broadway theatre and community centre from closure, Libby finally starts to remember the magic of Christmas. But she can't stop questioning her right to be happy when her parents are gone.

Can Harry convince Libby that she deserves her own Christmas miracle, or will she leave her heart -and her chance of happiness - in the Christmas shop at Central Park?

A Holly Bay Christmas

By Jo Bartlett

Maddie owns her dream business running a combined bookshop and tea rooms, in the beautiful Cornish village of Holly Bay. When Ben arrives looking for a place to rent, Maddie is keen to help him find a home in the town she loves, where they really know how to celebrate Christmas.

Stepping in to help Maddie raise money for a charity that's close to her heart, and even dressing as an elf on Christmas gift day, Ben seems too good to be true. Letting her guard down, she realises she's falling for the newcomer, but, when it turns out he's got a hidden agenda, she can't wait for him leave.

Will the storm that breaks out two days before Christmas, and cuts off Holly Bay from the rest of the world, give Ben another chance to prove himself to Maddie? Or is she destined to spend another Christmas with only her books for company?

Also available from Fabrian Books

Christmas at Spindlewood

By Zara Thorne

Laura Engleby loves Christmas; it's her favourite time of year. Her daughter, Holly, is due home from university; Spindlewood, their draughty but beautiful old house with its quirky turret, awaits its dressing up for the festive season; Cynthia, the Christmas tree fairy, is a vision in pink, and preparations are well in hand for Laura's Christmas Eve party, a tradition started in her late husband James's time, to which most of the residents of Charnley Acre are invited, and those who aren't turn up anyway.

When Clayton Masters, owner of Green and Fragrant Garden Services, finds himself with nowhere to sell his Christmas trees, Laura doesn't hesitate to let him use her garden. Christmas trees at Spindlewood – what could be more perfect? It's easy to overlook the fact that it's Spencer Jennings, the man Laura might just spend the rest of her life with, who is preventing Clayton from using his usual tree sales plot in the centre of the village. After all, it's just business. Isn't it?

Storm clouds gather above Spindlewood, threatening Laura's festive mood when she discovers that Clayton and Spencer are bitter enemies. She has no idea why, and nobody is saying, least of all the two men involved. Spencer's behaviour towards Clayton is as far from the spirit of the season as it could be, and Laura starts to wonder how well she really knows him. Clayton, on the other hand, behaves impeccably. What is more, it seems he will do anything for Laura.

When she realises that Clayton hates Christmas, Laura is shocked. How can anyone hate Christmas? But a much deeper shock is in store when she discovers the reason.

Laura is on a rescue mission – but what has Clayton's tragic story got to do with her, and why does his happiness matter so much to her?

Christmas at the Country Practice

By Sharon Booth

Christmas has arrived in Bramblewick, along with plenty of snow and festive good cheer. The village is gearing up for the Christmas Eve wedding of popular GP Connor Blake and much-loved receptionist Anna.

At the Bramblewick Surgery, a new GP, Riley McDonald, is working alongside Connor, and he's proving to be highly efficient and organised.

When Nell Williamson, proprietor of Spill the Beans café and bakery in the village, first sets eyes on Riley, it's love at first sight. Nell has always believed that she would know *the one* when she met him, and she's convinced that Riley is the man she's been waiting for.

Riley, on the other hand, is a hardened cynic. Having survived a humiliating broken engagement, he's keeping well away from relationships, and is confused by Nell's attentions.

Her every attempt to attract him pushes him further away, leaving Connor and Anna convinced she's on a hiding to nothing, even though he turns into a clumsy mess whenever Nell's around. Deciding she's a control freak who should be avoided at all costs, Riley makes a serious error of judgement which could cost her dearly.

Can the two of them reach an understanding before Connor and Anna's big day, or will it be the most awkward wedding in Bramblewick's history?

Christmas Wishes... New Year Kisses

By Pat Posner

From their very first meeting, sparks fly between Rose and Matthew. Discovering they have a lot in common – they are both coping with loss and both have a parentless child to love and care for – sometimes calms things and sometimes ignites those sparks further as they lend each other moral support through tough times. And though they both wish there could be a relationship between them, there are reasons there can't be.

It doesn't help that they're thrown together when their little nieces become best friends and want to see a lot of each other. There's fun and laughter and silly happenings when they spend time together. Neither Rose nor Matthew can they deny the little girls something that so clearly helps them – especially as Christmas is drawing near and memories can be painful.

But Christmas is a time for making wishes. But how can Christmas wishes come true for Rose and Matthew and the two little best friends?

Printed in Great Britain
by Amazon

35136594R00106